NW

PEPPER TREE RIDER

Center Point
Large Print

**This Large Print Book carries the
Seal of Approval of N.A.V.H.**

PEPPER TREE RIDER

Jack Curtis

CENTER POINT LARGE PRINT
THORNDIKE, MAINE

This Center Point Large Print edition
is published in the year 2019 by arrangement with
Golden West Literary Agency.

Copyright © 1994 by the Curtis Family Trust.

All rights reserved.

Originally published in the US by Walker and Co.

The text of this Large Print edition is unabridged.
In other aspects, this book may vary
from the original edition.
Printed in the United States of America
on permanent paper.
Set in 16-point Times New Roman type.

ISBN: 978-1-64358-338-9 (hardcover)
ISBN: 978-1-64358-342-6 (paperback)

Library of Congress Cataloging-in-Publication Data

The Library of Congress has cataloged this record
under Library of Congress Control Number: 2019943655

For top tree riders
Tyson and David,
Melissa and Mattis,
Oliver and Cyrus,
and
Haley Lynn.

Beware the fury of a patient man.

— Dryden

CHAPTER 1

THE OLD LACY-LEAVED pepper tree must have been there before the house was even built. Danny reckoned his dad had looked over the hot land spined with cactus, yucca, and mesquite, and decided that this one rare tree would always make welcome shade. Figuring how it would grow bigger with a little extra water, he probably had aimed the dog trot right at it so most of the house would lie in its shade when the south Texas summer sun was punishing all creatures living aboveground.

From that, anyone could surmise Harry Hamilton was a thoughtful and deliberate man, not easily stampeded and wise enough to use the few blessings nature offered.

The one thing he didn't figure on was the war. When word came that Colonel Hood needed volunteers for ninety days, he arranged for an old vaquero, Escudero Sanchez, to take care of his wife and son, then rode east over to Fort Sam Houston.

Years later the boy could not remember much about his father except the planed sunburned face.

The rest was what a lonely boy's imagination could make of his father. Danny envisioned him as big and strong because of the way the heavy logs had been raised up to make their house; and he'd be slow and careful in his judgment, because of the way he'd planned out not just the house but the corrals and the barn and the open-faced hay shed. He'd be a good man, because Danny's mama had married him, and he'd be plenty brave, because he'd come out ahead of the others and taken up new land even though the Comanches still came marauding on the hunting moons.

Before Hamilton left, he built a split-log bench that went clear around the trunk of the pepper tree—that act showed a sense of generosity and consideration for others, and Danny wondered if his papa realized at the time that his son would use the bench as the first step in climbing that fine old tree.

It wasn't done in a day. It took a year for the boy to work his way up from that bench into the topmost boughs. He used to climb to a safe fork, trim out the small branches, and consider himself a real bravo for coming up so far. Then maybe a couple weeks later, he'd see another fork farther on up.

By the time he reached the last crotch where he could build a platform of limbs covered with a bull's hide, he was big enough to help his mama with the chores and ride with Cisco whenever

Cisco's rheumatism let up enough for him to sit a horse.

The old vaquero worried about the work that wasn't being done, the calves that weren't cut and branded, the falling-down catch pens, the rawhide patching, all of the things that he and a helper would have attended to before his joints started to gravel him.

Cisco's wife had died early on from the fever, and he had put her in a special shrine in his heart, never looking for another woman to replace her. A long-waisted man with short bowed legs, he'd not been young when he sided with Hamilton. He'd ridden a lot of wild horses and a lot of miles, so it seemed predictable that he'd grow stiff and gray and spend a good deal of his time plaiting reatas or twisting *fiadors* from soft mane hair instead of bucking thorny brush after wild cattle.

Elizabeth Hamilton's younger brother, Lance, came over from Georgia to help out during the war, but he was more used to ordering slaves around than doing any work himself. With his fine golden hair falling to his silk neckerchief, and wearing pale blue pantaloons and a loosely pleated linen shirt, he looked more like a gambler or cotton speculator than a Texas rancher.

Lance Ballantine was thought to be weak in the chest, which was why he came over to the ranch instead of going to war. He was nervous, and as he'd never had to work with his body he wasn't especially strong and had a lot of problems with stomachaches, catarrh, asthma, fevers, and headaches. Elizabeth attributed his frailty to how he was raised on the plantation, and thanked her lucky stars Harry had come along and carried her off before she too settled into being delicate.

Elizabeth wasn't exactly a big, strong woman, but she pushed herself extra hard keeping the house and yard clean, taking care of the chickens, attending the milk cows, bucketing water to the rosebush and plum trees, then, at night, mending their clothes while Danny read the Bible aloud. Even after her husband had been gone three years, she never wore a dress that wasn't spotlessly clean.

"You never know, Danny," she said once, looking off to the east. "Your dad might ride in any time, and we sure wouldn't want him disappointed."

There was always that expectancy in her. Every time she'd look off down the eastern valley and see nothing but heat waves riding over the thorny brush, she'd force a smile, squint her eyes, and murmur, "He'll be along . . .

"It's not easy where he is," she'd say. "He'll be back as soon as he's finished up."

In the spring when the war ended and they heard of men making their way home, Danny took to watching down the valley from his platform high up in the pepper tree, wanting to be the first to see his daddy come riding home.

Through May and June he watched and waited, every morning thinking this would be the day and that when he saw him coming, he would holler down to his mama, "He's a-comin'!" and hurry down to the hard-packed dirt yard to greet him.

Lance spent more time playing monte in Sur Forks than he did with the boy. Old Cisco would listen to Danny, but he never talked much, even though he knew enough English to explain that mane hair made a better hackamore than tail hair because it was less scratchy, or why a rawhide reata had to be greased regularly with tallow to keep its life.

A mourning dove had built her nest on the other side of the pepper tree, and Danny heard her soft cooing as she also watched and waited down through the long summer days.

Once, the boy saw a rider approaching, and became so excited he nearly fell out of the tree. It turned out to be Lance. The boy didn't holler, and he didn't shinny down the tree, and he didn't even say hello when Lance rode into the yard, his thin features muddy green from some ailment. One time Cisco said Lance got that color from taking overmuch medicine.

Day after day the boy watched and waited as the clouds drifted over. Off in the cholla, a bull pawed the red dirt up over his shoulders and bellowed for a fight, and the mourning dove made her rhythmic cooing that weighed down the heavy noonday air.

From his perch Danny could watch his mama taking her bucket down to the barn or the well, or off somewhere. She was always carrying a bucket or basket, sometimes full, sometimes empty. Other times he watched Cisco kneeling in the yard in front of the bunkhouse, cutting strings from a flat cured cowhide.

Give him a hide and he could make anything he wanted, from watertight bags to fringed leggins, but his fingers were so knotted up now that he needed a lot of time.

Danny could see the flat country for miles around and the tree line where the south fork of the Sur roamed off to meet the north leg at Sur Forks.

"You, up there ridin' the pepper tree, be careful you don't get bucked off," Elizabeth would call up at him, smiling, not really worrying. She just wanted to say something that would help both of them stick it out through another day.

If she really wanted something done, she took on the tone of a bosslady and he knew he'd better do it or hunt a hole. She wasn't a very big lady, but she wasn't one to back down, and when she was plumb serious about making her wishes known, her blue eyes snapped like heat lightning, her reddish hair sparkled, and her cheeks flushed while her jaw set up firm as bedrock.

She never wore a sunbonnet the way other ladies did, because, she said, she liked the feel of the sun in her hair and be damned to the freckles on her nose.

Watching and waiting, Danny listened to the summer breeze riffling through the lacy leaves, while off in the brush a raven cawed at the empty sky and bobwhites whistled softly on the hard ground.

Sometimes a rider might come by, looking for work, and his mama would always turn him down, but offer him supper. She'd mention that Hamilton was coming back any day now, and the rider would go on his way.

Sometimes, after the rider left, Cisco would look worried and say, "We got to brand our cattle before some outsider does," but Elizabeth would answer, "Harry will see to it just as soon as he gets back," and Cisco would shake his head and grumble, "We're just askin' for trouble."

The men coming back from the war weren't the same as when they left, even if they were still in one piece, and quite a number weren't. A man with a black beard rode by one day, wearing a wooden peg leg that was contrived to fit into a hole in the bottom of his box stirrup, and another man, a young jasper with bitter features, held the reins of his horse in a cleft iron hook attached to his left forearm. Others were crippled so badly there wasn't anything left to strap a hook onto, or fit a wooden leg.

"It was the minié balls them Yankees threw at us," the black-bearded man told Danny. "Before the minié balls, the old smooth-bore muskets would send a lead ball through your body and it might kill you, but it'd not often shatter the bones. The minié balls come so hard and fast, they just splatter anything they hit."

Danny hoped his daddy was never hit with a minié ball and had worried on it ever since the black-bearded man left.

Saturdays Elizabeth and the boy generally took the buckboard into Sur Forks for supplies. She would trade cheese and eggs in the Mercantile for Arbuckles coffee, cornmeal, flour, salt, and sorghum molasses, but sometimes she'd have to throw in one of Cisco's reatas to make the trade even.

The storekeeper, Martin Weissgut, was a smiling fat man with a short, bristly mustache who always wore a bloody apron. Mr. Weissgut had come into Texas with a colony of Germans, but he never liked farming and moved farther west, where he could trade goods.

His store was on the corner. Across the street to the east was the Merry Widow Saloon, run by old Tom Fortune, then kitty-corner was Joab Vibor's brick bank. Joab Vibor, a new man in town, had somehow bought the bank away from Colonel Ashbery, who had fought in the Mexican war.

Down the street, another brick building held the jail and Marshal Ogden Gant's office.

From the central square, the town drifted off toward the empty land, petering out after two or three blocks.

It was here on the streets of Sur Forks where you could see the effects of the minié ball. Half the men sitting on benches along the boardwalk were shy a hand, forearm, arm, foot, or leg. These men weren't much good for hard work, so they did odd jobs and sat their lives out in the small town, watching and waiting much the same as Danny did in the pepper tree.

Most times the boy was too afraid of the town kids to leave his mama and go off on his own. Town kids dressed different and acted different and they traveled together, so a loner like him didn't have much of a chance if they took to hazing him. His mama said it was perfectly safe in town, and Danny did reckon he could whip anyone near his size, but he wasn't so sure about a whole gang of them.

The girls were worse because they poked their noses up in the air when he passed by, like he was smelly, which after a bath in the copper boiler in the middle of the kitchen he knew he wasn't.

Still, there they were, pigtails and ribbons, shiny shoes and lace collars, passing by hand in hand, noses up like coyotes ready to sing at the moon.

Before Elizabeth did anything else, she always went into the Mercantile to ask Mrs. Weissgut if there was any mail.

Mrs. Weissgut would look in the box marked H for Hamilton, maybe riffle through a couple of envelopes that she'd already looked at, then shake her head and say, "Sorry."

Then Elizabeth would go over to Mr. Weissgut and tell him, "My wagon is out back with my goods," and he'd send out a couple of crippled men to bring in her produce.

Meantime she'd give Mr. Weissgut her list, and he'd sack it all up; the same maimed men would carry out the supplies.

After the trading was all done, she and Danny would walk up and down the streets for a while, looking to see if anything had changed, then they'd stop in at Maggie's Cafe for a piece of fresh-baked pie.

Elizabeth knew most of the folks and would listen to the gossip, always trying to find out what was happening to the soldiers. One time, before the war's end, she stopped to speak to old Marshal Gant sitting in front of the town jail. Danny was deathly afraid of his long white mustache, hard, craggy features, and cold blue eyes.

"Have you heard anything from your son, Mr. Gant?" she asked.

"Yes, ma'am." Marshal Gant nodded somberly. "I received a letter from his captain saying Albert was killed over by Nashville."

"I'm so very sorry," Elizabeth murmured, like she'd been kicked by a mule. "What a mortal shame."

"It's a costly war," Marshal Gant said. "I wish it were me instead of him."

"He was such a good boy," Elizabeth said, touching the old man's bony shoulder with a gesture that said it better than words.

Watching and waiting, Danny played the spy in the treetop, sighting over enemy lines, imagining General Forrest's cavalry charging across the land at Federal troops in blue, overrunning them and capturing all the flags before galloping away.

Other times, he pretended to be the deadliest of sharpshooters with his long-barreled rifle loaded with minié balls, picking out General Sherman from among his adjutants, taking aim at his fearsome red-bearded visage, picking a spot right between his bulging, mad eyes.

"Why doesn't he come?" he nagged his mama at mealtimes. "Lots of them are back and fixing to leave again."

"It's a far piece to Georgia," she said. "He's doing as best a man can do."

"Maybe he's bad hurt," Danny suggested innocently.

"Hush you down, Danny," she said in her

bosslady voice. "We will not think that way. He will return. He'll be tired and maybe even hungry, but he'll be all in one piece and able to ride along with pride."

"He could write, couldn't he?"

"Of course, child!" she cried out sweetly. "And no doubt he has, but likely his letters have been lost in all the confusion."

All they knew for sure was that he started out in Hood's brigade, and that he had been in Georgia, fighting General Sherman.

Early in July during the heat of the day when even the range bulls had quit their bellowing and retreated to the mesquite's shade, Danny lay on his perch high over the ranch yard and saw a faint plume of dust rising off to the east.

It might have been a dust devil, except it stayed steady on the trail. It wasn't Lance, because he was stretched out on a bench under the brush arbor. Of course, it could be anyone.

Whoever it was, he rode slow and steady. A wagon or buggy would have made more dust than a lone rider, and Danny settled in his mind that this time it had to be his daddy.

Still, he couldn't call out, "He's a-comin'," without being sure.

Through the heat waves the rider came on, steady and strong. He was tall, and sat the saddle straight up, but not bending over backward to prove the point.

Even then, Danny held off hollering.

Tall and enduring, he came on until Danny could see the gray Kossuth hat with the brim let down, the gray shirt and trousers, the steady trot of the big gray horse.

It had to be him.

He came riding, gray as the mourning dove. Gray as the dust. Gray as Lee's lost armies.

Danny couldn't see the rider's face for the grayness, but the boy couldn't think he was anybody other than his dad. Joyfully, Danny leaned down into the yard and yelled at his mama in the summer kitchen, "He's a-comin'!"

"Oh, lordy, Danny, you about scared the piewaddin' out of me," Elizabeth called back after a second. She came over to the pepper tree as Danny came scooting down.

"How do you know?" she asked, the quiver in her voice betraying her as she put both hands to her forehead and peered off to the east.

"It's him," he cried out. "He's a tall man on a big gray, and he's wearin' a Reb uniform."

"But you couldn't know for sure," she said, clutching his shoulder with her left hand, gazing off at the distant rider.

"Nobody else like him ever rode out this way," he said defensively. "It has to be him."

Lance came out from under the brush arbor and rubbed the sleep out of his eyes. "Harry?" he asked anxiously.

21

"Lord knows. I surely hope so," she said, her breath coming quicker as she tried to calm herself.

"I was afraid . . ." Lance didn't finish.

"Well, lordy, so was I, but we always knew no harm would come to him," Elizabeth quavered joyfully.

"Why don't he hurry on in?" Danny asked, the excitement riding high in him.

"He would never abuse a horse in this kind of heat," she said. "It's just like him."

"Don't get your hopes up too much," Lance said. "It could just be some saddle bum looking for a free meal."

"They don't ride like that man rides," she said, breathless now. "Oh my, I haven't done the baking yet!"

"Be careful, Elizabeth," Lance said. "Wait till you're sure."

Tall and implacable, the rider came on across the burnt plain as if he'd come a thousand miles and had another thousand to go. Rising and falling in the heat waves, and gray as the mourning dove, he came on.

Danny kept trying to make out his face but somehow he couldn't. It was like the dust had covered him in gray flannel.

"Oh, please God," Elizabeth said, afraid now because she couldn't make out the rider's face either.

"I don't think it's him," Lance said.

"You don't know!" she answered angrily.

"He should wave or something," Danny said.

"It's Harry," she said. "It has to be. If there's a God in heaven, it's him."

"Please, Elizabeth," Lance said, touching her shoulder, "if it's not, it'll be tomorrow or the next day."

"Oh, God," she whispered and covered her eyes for a second as he rode into the yard.

They all stared up at him. Elizabeth was the only one of them who'd recognize him for sure and she wasn't speaking, only staring up at the tall man wearing a gray flannel cloth tied over most of his face.

There was a scar running out from under the cloth up close to his left eye. A lump of scar tissue, still red, nudged out below the eyebrow or what was left of it.

"The Lazy H ranch?" he asked quietly, and Danny's heart sank because his dad wouldn't need to ask.

"Harry?" Elizabeth asked, even though she was almost sure he was not her husband.

"My name is Dave Cameron, ma'am. I have some news of Harry, but I'd like to water my horse first."

"Oh dear," she fussed, "I was expecting Harry and forgot my manners. Light down, mister, water your horse, and come sit with us."

23

Danny waited for him to drop the gray cloth down off his face, but he didn't.

After watering his horse, he tethered him in the shade and came back to where they were still standing.

"Come in out of the sun," Elizabeth said in a tired voice. "I'll fix some coffee and find some sweet bread."

Dave Cameron nodded and followed them over to the brush arbor, where a big plank table and benches waited for days just like this one . . .

"Please take a seat," she said, staring at the covered face and mismatched eyes.

"After you, ma'am. I'm sorry, but my news is not what I'd like to be bringing. The boy . . . ?"

"Danny's all right." She settled down on the bench and put her hands over her eyes. "Go ahead," she murmured. "Is he alive?"

"No, ma'am," Cameron said after a moment. "He fought as brave as the bravest . . . and suffered no pain."

CHAPTER 2

THE MOURNING DOVE in the pepper tree kept on with its sad cooing as if nothing had happened, and Danny felt like throwing a rock at the fool bird.

His mother had gone into the house, walking unsteadily, but resisting any help from Lance or Dave Cameron.

"I'll just be a minute," she had said carefully. "I'd like some time to collect myself, if you please."

Even though Danny wanted to run and hide, he stared at the stranger who looked like Danny's image of an avenging angel from the Book of Revelations. That's who Dave Cameron was. The Bible said there was no escaping the angel.

Cameron moved toward Danny, reaching out his hand as if to take the boy by the shoulder, but Danny darted quickly to the dog trot. Looking over his shoulder, he saw Cameron wasn't after him. Cameron had turned and was facing Lance.

The boy stopped and waited, ready to flee, but wanting to hear what else Cameron had to say about his dad.

"Maybe I should have waited until the boy was gone," Cameron told Lance.

"He had to hear it from somebody," Lance said, stroking his fine silky mustache and sitting down at the table. "You were with Harry when he was hit?"

"We fought almost three years together without a scratch until a canister of grape blew up in front of us."

"Must have been hard," Lance said politely, as if he'd heard the same story a hundred times.

"It's past," Cameron said. "Somehow we've got to start over."

"Where you from?" Lance asked.

"Nowhere anymore. The ranch down in Bee County is gone to a carpetbagger banker. My folks died before I joined up."

"There's nothing for you here," Lance said, looking off at the empty plain.

"Excuse me, I wasn't meaning to ask for charity. I'm not that bad off."

"I wasn't saying that, I just meant we have nothing to offer. Times are hard."

A gust of wind spun through the yard, rattling several loose shakes on the roof, and Cameron looked around at the sagging corral fence scabbed with scraps of wood and held together with rawhide bindings. The door on the blacksmith shop canted to one side. The winch over the well was broken and leaned off the coping so that water had to be bucketed up on a rope by hand. A flatbed wagon was missing a wheel. A single-wall outbuilding had completely collapsed into a rough pile of gray boards.

"I can see that," Cameron said. "I'd work for free if it'd help you folks out."

"I can handle it," Lance said. "The asthma cripples me once in a while so I can't make a big show of the placc, but I do just fine."

"I was just offering," Cameron said stiffly. "I reckon I'll be on my way."

Turning toward Danny, he called out, "I'm sorry if I upset you, son. Sometimes when it comes to death, there's no other way."

"I know who you are," Danny flared, and started to run into the kitchen, but his mother was coming out and caught him.

Her eyes were red, but she kept her head up and her voice was firm. "What's the trouble, Danny?"

"He killed Dad!" the boy piped out, near to panic. "Now he wants to kill us!"

"Hush now, child," Elizabeth said, drawing him close to her. "Mr. Cameron was a close friend of your father and has gone out of his way to clear up all our doubts and worries. For that, we owe him a debt of gratitude."

"He's Death!" Danny yelled. "Death on a Pale Horse, just like the Bible says!"

"No, son, he's only a mortal man travelin'

27

through this world of woe," she said, stroking his head. "You mustn't be afraid."

"I promised I'd come," Cameron said. "I'm sorry it has to be this way."

"We all must face the truth," Elizabeth said softly. "We'd like you to stay awhile and maybe talk about Harry's last times, how it was with him."

"Uncle Lance told him to git on," Danny said fiercely.

"I surely hope that's an exaggeration," she said, glancing at Lance. Then she turned to Cameron and said, "You're most welcome to stay as long as you like."

"That's mighty kind of you, ma'am," Dave Cameron said, "but I reckon I better mosey along."

"Mr. Cameron, my brother hates to admit it, but he's been poorly for some time. Sometimes he feels embarrassed and as a consequence says things he wouldn't otherwise say." Elizabeth was looking at Dave Cameron, but it was clear that she was talking to Lance.

Her brother's face flushed red. "I just told him we had no money," Lance muttered.

"But, Lance, dear," she chided him gently, "no one has money. We're all in the briar patch together, and we must help each other out as best we can!"

"Ma'am, I don't want to be the cause of a

family dispute," Cameron said. "If you have no need of an extra hand, I'll be traveling on."

"That's right," Lance said sharply. "There's no need, and no money. That's what I said."

"But what about the heavy work around here, and the catch pens over by the river that are falling down? What about all the cattle that must be branded? My goodness, I can see a mountain of work, if Mr. Cameron will forego wages until there's a market for the cows."

Breathing hoarsely, Lance went into a coughing fit where he seemed unable to get air into his lungs. Elizabeth went over, leaned down, and held him in both arms until he could get his breath.

"My goodness, Lance, I surely didn't mean to upset you so much. Now, just calm down, it's going to be all right . . ."

"It'll never be all right so long as you don't let me run things my way," Lance choked out, and went off into the house. When he reached the door that opened into the bedrooms, he turned back and said hoarsely, "I said I didn't want any help, and I don't!"

With that he went inside, slamming the door behind him.

"That's pretty plain, ma'am," Cameron said, backing away.

"No, sir, it is not as plain as it seems," she said strongly. "My brother may not want any help, but he surely does need it. We both do. If you're willing, I'd like you to help gather the cattle."

"How many critters out there?" Cameron asked quietly.

"Goodness knows. I'd hoped when . . . Harry . . . came back, we could start the roundup and find out what we've got and what we haven't."

"Are they on open range?"

"Yes, but our neighbors and we are accustomed to using certain parts of it. In general, we consider the range between the ranch and the river ours. On the other side of the river to the rimrock belongs to Drum Biggers. Back the other way from us, Pat Hare's cattle graze in the Peachtree Creek basin."

"When was the last time you had a roundup?"

"Not since Dad went off to war," Danny piped up, figuring the stranger was asking too many questions.

"There'll be considerable increase," Cameron said, nodding.

"You can see Lance is in no condition for hard work, and old Cisco is not the rider he used to be, so we've had to just let them run free."

"Your neighbors could have helped," Cameron suggested.

"No, we're all shorthanded and out of cash," Elizabeth said. "We've just been waiting for the day the men . . . came home."

30

"You look awful old," Danny said out of the blue.

"Hush now, Danny," Elizabeth said. "Mind your manners."

"I'm twenty-eight," Cameron told the boy. "How about you?"

"I'm almost ten."

"Have a pony?" Cameron asked mildly.

Danny only nodded. Topsy, loafing in the corral, was a perfectly built quarter horse, except for some reason he was a runt. He was smart, and though he couldn't keep up with the bigger horses, he was plenty strong.

"Ride much?" the soldier asked.

Again Danny nodded, looking at the ground.

"Danny, speak up to the man when he asks you a civil question," Elizabeth said, smoothing out his hair. "Likely he can teach you a lot about the cattle business."

"That's all right, ma'am," Cameron said. "They say still water runs deep."

"Will you stay, Mr. Cameron?" she asked, looking at him square on.

"I'll help through your roundup and the branding. After that, we'll see."

"Fine," Elizabeth said. "There's no one in the bunkhouse except Cisco, and I'm sure he'll value your company. He speaks some English."

"*Bueno*," Cameron replied, an odd trace of laughter touching his voice.

"You come up and eat with us soon as you're settled in," she said.

"You don't have to . . . do this," Cameron said softly.

"Mr. Cameron, if there's one single thing I have to do, it is exactly this," she said. Then she gave Danny a little push and said, "Introduce Mr. Cameron to Cisco, Danny. Make him feel at home."

Elizabeth called upon every bit of her faith to find the strength to get through that hour. She should have been off wailing her heart out, but somehow she knew that this stranger was the most important person in their lives and so she put aside her grief to welcome him.

As for Danny, he had been afraid of Cameron from the moment he saw the mask. Keeping a safe distance, he led Cameron along the corral down to the bunkhouse, which wasn't much more than a cabin with room for four wooden bunks inside. Wooden crates nailed to the walls served for storage. Oilskin slickers, worn chaps, a dusty hat, an empty saddlegun scabbard, and odds and ends of workingmen's clothing hung from spikes. In the center was an iron potbellied stove for heat in the winter. A couple of rawhide-mended chairs and a table made all the comforts of home.

Cisco sat as usual on the south-side bench, where he was in the sun but out of the wind, working at plaiting soft leather strips that would probably end up as a fancy headstall.

He looked up, his dark eyes curious, saw the man in the gray mask, and nodded. He didn't flinch or stare.

"Afternoon, sir."

"Call me Dave," Cameron said, extending his hand.

"Cisco. Please to meet you," the old vaquero replied. He extended a hand that had four fingers but just a stub of a thumb.

"*Mocho*. Dallying a turn?" Dave Cameron asked, shaking the maimed hand.

"Yes, the young bull was quicker than I expected." Cisco shrugged and smiled. "I was learning like Danny then."

"We all must learn."

Danny noticed that Cisco wasn't afraid of the stranger.

The vaquero glanced at the mask and asked, "The war?"

"Yes."

"So it is." Cisco shrugged again, shaking his head. "And Harry?"

"Dead."

"What a pity," Cisco murmured, then spread both hands out wide and added, "*ni modo*."

"Yes," Cameron nodded. "There is no answer, no solution, no nothing."

"You wish to stay here?"

"If you don't mind, I'll take one of the bunks."

33

"No, no problem." Cisco held up his hands. "¡*Bienvenidos*!"

The three of them went inside, and Cameron tossed his bedroll on a bunk by the window. He looked around a second, then said, "It's some better'n I'm used to."

They heard a horse coming out of the corral. Danny looked through the window and saw that it was Lance on his roan. He was dressed for town.

"Kind of late to be leaving, isn't it?" Cameron said.

"It's his business," Danny snapped out, annoyed by the stranger's nosiness.

"True enough, Danny," Cameron murmured as they walked back up to the house with Cisco, who was using a cane he'd made of ironwood and then served with thinnest cut rawhide.

"You goin' to work the cattle?" Cisco asked, pegging along.

Cameron nodded. "I figure to look the ground over tomorrow."

"Last time I rode clear to the river, somebody took a shot at me," Cisco said. "Maybe it was some hunter that made a mistake, maybe not."

"Can you still ride?"

"Some," Cisco said, grinning, "but it's finding the stirrup that's hardest."

"I'll put you in the saddle, *viejo*," Cameron said. "All you have to do is stay there."

34

"Your face ever goin' to heal?" Cisco asked plain out.

"¡*Ojalá*!" Cameron put his hands together and rolled his eyes heavenward as the old vaquero chuckled.

"Does that mean it will?" Danny asked quickly.

"It means I'm still hoping, Danny."

"You look like the angel of death to me," the boy blurted out.

"You seen a lot of death, Danny?" Cameron asked in that mild, quiet tone.

"No."

"Count your blessings then," he said quietly.

It was still hot enough to eat outside, and Elizabeth cooked in what she called her summer kitchen, which was only the back part of the brush arbor where a broken-down cast-iron stove sat with makeshift lids and an oven door that had to be hooked shut with a wire. Next to it was a knocked-together table and a couple of packing boxes for her pots and pans. Cooking out there was a good deal cooler than being inside with a hot stove going.

Besides the usual steak and beans, she'd made some biscuits to sop up the bean juice, and along with the biscuits she'd fried a sorghum cake for dessert. It was simple fare, but she always managed to get the best flavor out of the most common grub. Cameron cleaned his plate right off.

"I like to see a man eat," she said, filling up his plate again.

Danny watched him. Cameron ate funny, slipping the food under the mask and into his mouth, then chewing on one side. The boy wondered if he had any teeth or even any jaw left on the other side, but this time he stifled the impulse to ask.

Cameron would stick his little finger out and push the gray flannel away from his mouth just as the fork came up. Likely he'd had a lot of practice.

He wasn't in any pain, or at least he didn't seem to be. Of course, wearing a mask, there wasn't much of a way anyone could tell if it hurt him to eat or not. It sure didn't hold him back anyway.

If it were me, Danny thought, I'd likely just take a plate and go sit on the back steps, take off the mask, and eat like a dog.

When they'd finished the sorghum cake and were sitting around waiting for the sun to go down, Cameron asked Cisco, "Have you any idea how many cattle are between here and the river?"

"I can only guess. We had more than a thousand head at the last roundup, not countin' calves."

"They increase at least by half every year, so that'd make . . . maybe four or five thousand head."

"Maybe more," Cisco said, nodding. "The grass has been good. The grizzlies are gone."

"What do you figure they'd sell for, Cisco?"

"Around here you can make more money just shootin' them for their hides," the old vaquero said, shaking his head.

"There's a railroad moving west from Missouri, Cisco. Suppose we drove a couple thousand up there?"

"You might get six dollars a head. But you might get killed too." Cisco shrugged. "Somebody up toward San Antonio tried it. They lost the whole herd and half the men to Missouri bushwhackers."

"They're crying for beef in the East. Someone's going to figure a way to get it there and make a profit," Cameron said. "It just needs studying."

"What are you talking about," Elizabeth asked, coming back to the table, "driving these crazy longhorns all the way to Missouri?"

"That's the only way they're worth hard money," Cameron said. "Suppose you took a herd up to Kansas and wintered 'em over on free grass?"

"But who would buy them?" she asked.

"A Kansas Pacific railroad is working its way west. Come spring, you could have your herd up there fat as butter just waiting for the train."

"You're talking a lot of months from now," she said. "It's too late this year to make the gather and drive too. You'd have to wait till early spring."

"The cattle would gain weight just grazing along, going slow," Cameron persisted.

"Why not put a railroad to right here?" Danny asked, caught up in the newfound sense of hope.

"It takes money," Cameron said, "and right now there's none left in the South."

"Did Harry tell you about the mortgage?" Elizabeth asked, frowning.

"Men sitting around a campfire, waiting for battle, talk," Cameron said, nodding. "He figured the banker would be lenient because of the war."

"Joab Vibor is new here and not inclined toward leniency," she said, not smiling. For the first time, Danny began to understand how important the haggling with Mr. Weissgut was every Saturday.

"How are you paying the interest?" Cameron asked.

"With cattle," Elizabeth said. "Every year I give him a promissory note on three hundred cows valued at two dollars a head."

"That's not right." Cameron's voice took on some heat. "They're worth two or three times that."

"He's got me whipsawed," she said, her face showing worry.

The sun, setting a lurid red in the west, lit a fire on Cameron's masked face.

"I can go talk to this man Vibor," he said quietly.

"No, Mr. Cameron, it'd be a favor to me if

you'd just ride out and make sure the cattle really are out on the range where they should be."

"*Más vale prevenir que lamentar*," Cisco muttered.

"Yes, it *is* better to protect than to cry," Cameron said, looking at Cisco, "What's wrong? Why do you think we need protection?"

"I don't know for sure," Cisco shook his head. "Sometimes I think I hear noises that don't belong over there."

"Lance has ridden our range to the west and found nothing unusual," Elizabeth said.

"Then why are you uneasy about it, ma'am?" Cameron asked.

"My brother would do anything for me," Elizabeth said hesitantly. "It's just that . . . lately, he's changed."

"Changed how?"

"He's got his head in the clouds, doesn't want to talk seriously. Maybe he's fallen in love, or something."

"Why not ask him?"

"Because I want him to stand on his own, Mr. Cameron," she said. "I want him to make his own decisions."

"Then it won't hurt to take a look over yonder just in case."

"In case?" She frowned.

"In case he's so moonstruck, he can't count cows."

CHAPTER 3

IN THAT PART of the country, the time for doing was early morning, when the air was cool and fresh with dew: after midday, the sun would be close overhead, pressing the life out of the people, so that anything sensible hunted for shade and waited until the sun yawed westward and started to peter out.

It was Elizabeth's custom to rise before daybreak and have the breakfast on the table early enough so that a full working day could be got in before the heat drove everyone to cover.

The air was always sweetest then: the plant life's breathing in the night left a delicate perfume floating over the cool, pale blue land. That sweet dawn air had a power of its own that made a person feel fine and strong.

Elizabeth would sometimes exclaim, "My! What a grand morning!"

Danny would say, "It makes me hungry."

And on this morning, Dave Cameron said, "It doesn't seem real, the way the light and the air fit together."

Cisco murmured, "*Así es*."

And Elizabeth gave them boiled grits with raw sugar and thick cream.

"I made some extra," she said to Cameron, filling his bowl again, "figuring you been underfed for a while."

"We were seldom short on parched corn," Cameron replied, his scarred left eye twinkling, "and it was at least filling."

"You mean that's all you had to eat in the war?" Danny asked, his caution suppressed by curiosity.

"Not always," Cameron said. "Sometimes we'd capture a wagonload of hard biscuit."

"You're fooling," Danny said.

"A little." He nodded, and looked up questioningly at Elizabeth. "Where's your brother?"

"I'm not sure." She looked away.

"He didn't come home last night," Danny said. His uncle's bunk was right across the room from Danny's.

"Should we go looking for him?" Cameron asked, frowning.

He was trying to be polite and not ask the hard question, but it was clear that he needed to know what was going on.

"No, don't worry about it," she said, bending over the stove, her back to him. "Sometimes he stays in town."

"Lots of times," Danny said.

"It's his business, Danny," she came back at him. "You watch yourself."

"I was just counting the crew," Cameron said, trying to smooth it over. "I reckon we won't wait on him."

"No." Elizabeth tried to force a laugh. "Don't wait on his account. My brother's not irresponsible, but he's young, and he's been sickly all his life—on top of that, he was raised different."

She was talking a lot just to cover up her disappointment. Anyone could see it, but she did it anyway.

"You mean he had a different upbringing than you?"

"Not exactly, Mr. Cameron." She turned around. "We had the same family and the same house and servants and all, but I ran off from it and he didn't."

"No offense, ma'am, but why did either one of you leave such a good life?"

"It's no secret, Mr. Cameron. Harry and I met in Atlanta before the war, and I discovered I wanted to be alongside him more than I wanted to sit at home and drink lemonade all day." She smiled, remembering.

"And Lance?"

"Well, now—" She turned apologetic again. "He does like his lemonade . . ."

"I understand, ma'am," he said, getting to his feet.

Suddenly it occurred to Danny that Cameron never called her Mrs. Hamilton. It was just a small thing, but it stuck in his head even though he didn't know what to make of it.

Cisco, Cameron, and Danny filed out toward the corral, where the horses snuffled at bits of straw on the ground while watching them out of the corners of their eyes.

There was no need to rope any of them because they were well-trained saddle horses. Topsy came right over to Danny because he knew the boy would have a dab of sugar for him.

Topsy was small enough that Danny could slip the bridle over his ears and buckle the throat latch, but Danny wasn't quite big enough to put on the saddle by himself.

Cisco had made the saddle for Danny, and after the boy had smoothed the blanket on Topsy's back, Cisco set the saddle in place, and let Danny cinch up the leathers while he went after his own gelding, a strong, long-legged sorrel.

He preferred the medium-weight hackamore to a bridle for that horse, and while the sorrel made a show of backing up, he didn't make any bad moves when Cisco tossed the horsehair *fiador* over his neck, the signal for him to stand steady.

"I'll help you with the saddle, Cisco," Cameron said. He smoothed out the blanket and topped it with an old slick fork with a big apple horn, then let Cisco tighten his Spanish rig cinch.

While Cameron was saddling his big gray, Cisco tucked his walking stick under the fender,

43

took the big horn in his gnarled old left hand, and tried to get his boot into the hickory box stirrup, but the knee wouldn't bend enough and he gave it up.

"I'm damned if I'm goin' to stand on a stump," he said fiercely, mad at himself.

"Up you go," Cameron said, and putting both hands around the old vaquero's waistband, lifted him up like a bag of straw and set him down gently onto the saddle.

Cisco had to grin even though he was angry at his knees. His boots found the familiar tapaderos and he was pleased to once again be where he liked best.

The three of them rode out the gate and waved goodbye to Elizabeth just as the sun came up in the east in a flood of crimson light.

Danny had a faint recollection of his dad setting him up on a saddle like Cameron had just done Cisco. He remembered sitting up so high in the air it seemed a mile, and being nervous, but excited too. Then while his mama put a hand up to keep him from falling off, his dad led the big gelding around the corral. When they'd made the circle, his dad reached up and put him down on the ground again. He smiled, his ruddy sunburned face crinkling the weather lines, his eyes pleased as he ruffled Danny's hair. He seemed like a giant, a friendly giant . . .

Between the ranchhouse and the river were

several miles of broken range, some of it small grassy valleys and some of it rocky mesquite and cactus country where the longhorns liked to hide out in the day, then graze on the grasslands at night.

As they rode along, Cisco pointed out the familiar landmarks and named them—Eagle Rock, Loma Prieta, Pigbone Valley, Pilgrim Point, La Tinaja, Organ Pipe Bluff—so that Cameron could come to know the country quicker.

They rode at a fast walk in the fresh morning until Cameron saw movement in a mesquite thicket and said, "There's critters in there I want to see," and kicked the gray ahead.

Charging the thicket, he spooked out five longhorns of assorted colors and sizes, and rode up alongside them before turning back.

"A young bull, unbranded, and four cows, two of them branded Lazy H," he said when he returned.

"That's about right," Cisco said, nodding.

They went on that way awhile longer, with Cameron chousing out an occasional group of wild cattle to check their brands or see if they were still unbranded.

"Seems like there ought to be more," he muttered.

Cisco said, "Maybe better close to the river."

Danny wondered if someday Cameron would tell him how he and his dad had met and what they'd done together for three years. The boy imagined his dad riding up an open hillside covered with wounded men and saving Dave Cameron's life. That's probably how they met, Danny thought—Cameron was crying for water on the open hillside in the hot sun as the cowardly Yankees poured their fire down from behind a stone wall, and Dad rode out and carried Dave to safety in the trees, with minié balls whistling all around . . .

Danny noticed Cameron still wasn't carrying a gun. Cisco didn't have a gun either, but he always kept a big bowie scabbarded to his belt. He could do just about anything with that bowie, from shaving every Saturday to carving a saddle tree, and the boy figured if anybody ever made Cisco mad, he'd rip him from crotch to brisket right quick.

No one talked much as they searched for cattle. Danny had a vague recollection of his dad shushing him one time when they took a little ride into the mesquite country. He did it by reaching over and putting his big, rope-calloused hand over the boy's jabbering mouth.

After that he quit making unnecessary noises riding the wild country, and after a while, he learned that the quieter you went, the more you saw—things like deer and peccaries, coyotes, lynx, foxes, and bobcats.

Once Danny understood the value of silence,

he worked at it. Not just the talking, but keeping his pony on quiet grass, taking the jingles off his bridle, tallowing the leathers to hold down the creaking. It gave him pleasure to come up on a litter of coyote pups playing with their mama or get close enough to watch the wild turkeys doing a mating dance.

The way the mesquite thickets lay caused the riders to spread out, each following his own path westward. Danny could still catch a glimpse of the other two as they wound their way through the prickly country and there was no concern about getting lost, because the big landmarks were in plain sight. They were spooking out more and more cattle as Cisco had promised. Cameron would ride close, check their hides, and let them go. Topsy wasn't enough horse to handle the big, mossy-horned critters and stayed clear of them.

Danny knew how quick and strong they were and how they used their long horns to hook and stab, and he'd heard the tale of a battle between a longhorn bull and a full-grown grizzly bear, with the longhorn coming out the winner; of how they'd hook a slow horse's guts out if given any chance at all; of how they'd battle each other from sunup to sundown.

He should have known better than to ride between two thickets of dense mesquite making a crooked tunnel.

He was daydreaming instead of thinking as

little Topsy walked through that overhanging spiny growth when Danny saw the lineback grulla bull coming from the other way, his head lowering.

The boy tried to spin Topsy on a dime and did well enough, but Topsy made a break through a little side trail, turning so quick Danny was off balance, then a mesquite limb caught him under the chin and lifted him clear of his stirrups.

The boy was hanging onto the limb with both hands when the bull lunged blindly by.

The bull turned his head up, looking around for the boy, and Danny swung back and forth, trying to catch the mesquite limb with his spurs.

The bull saw Danny about the same time he hooked his right leg over the limb, but the boy's weight bent the limb down, just about horn high.

Forgetting about the thorns clawing at his face, Danny swung on up to straddle the limb.

The bull charged. Danny saw his red eyes, his swollen neck, and his needle sharp horns, ringed and mossy where they anchored into his skull, and figured he was a goner.

The big gray horse came in from the side and hit the bull with its shoulder hard enough to knock him down, then Cameron reached over and grabbed the boy out of the tree as he guided the gray with his knees clear of the bull.

Danny felt like crying, but he didn't.

"Why didn't you yell?" Cameron asked as

Danny worked his way around so he was behind, holding on to the big man's waist.

"I forgot."

They found Cisco in a grassy clearing, holding Topsy's reins. "I hope you didn't hurt that bull," Cisco said to the boy.

"We broke even," Danny muttered as he slid off the gray and climbed back aboard his pony.

"That bull had a Windowpane brand on his butt," Cameron said, giving the gray a breather. "His earmark was a full crop."

"I never see that brand before," Cisco said.

"Could be a stray from anywhere," Cameron said.

"I been around here too long. Maybe I'm just getting too old," Cisco said, shaking his head, "but I keep thinking somethin's wrong."

"I reckon it'll turn up, whatever it is," Cameron said.

"Maybe you ought to be wearing a gun," Danny spoke up.

"No more," Cameron said curtly, looking hard at the boy.

As they started off, Danny wished for the thousandth time he'd known his dad better and how he handled things, how he would speak to a man who said, "No more." Would he let it lie, or would he ask, "Why the hell not?"

Sometimes the boy talked to his dad inside his head, but it wasn't the same as if he were hunkered down alongside him, scratching in the dirt with a stick . . .

"Maybe you oughta be wearin' a gun, Dad."

"Maybe you're right, son. I could have shot that grulla bull instead of putting my horse that close to his horns."

"And there might be some Comanches comin' down the river."

"I didn't think about that. I'm sure glad you're sidin' me, son."

"Two pullin' together is better'n one."

"Maybe I can find you one of those new .36-caliber Navy Colts. Be just about your size."

"I'd appreciate that, Dad."

Cisco led them through some large oaks and junipers into a little valley that ended in a box canyon where his dad and Cisco had built their wild-cattle catch pen. Made of close-set posts and rails, the fence extended out about six feet, right at the head of the canyon. The trap consisted of a single, one-way trigger leading into a gullet that could be stopped off by a gate between the pen and the box canyon. At one of the outlets from the gullet was a chute that squeezed down so that a critter could be marked and branded.

Danny had seen it a while back, when Cisco could ride, but even then it had started to fall apart from disuse and weather. The main trigger entrance was two gates made of sharpened laddered pickets that angled inward. Usually they were held loosely together by wires hanging down from an overhead arch so that cattle could shoulder through for salt or water but would not be able to push back out when the sharpened pickets swung together.

Danny remembered that some of the hanging wires had rusted away, leaving a gap in the triggering gates, and that some of the fence had been down.

Riding up close, he could see the fences had been repaired with lengths of rawhide and the trigger gates had been rehung with new wire.

All around were cattle tracks and cow splatter, and inside the box canyon were a few longhorns.

"Stout trap," Cameron said, looking at the triggers and outlet chute.

"It's ours," Danny said feistily.

"I didn't think I could hear this far," Cisco said, "but that's what I heard. Somebody working cattle over here."

Nobody had to say rustlers. That's all it could be.

"With beef only worth two or three dollars a head," Cameron asked, "why would anyone go to all the trouble?"

"It don't make a never-mind," Danny said. "They're stealin' our cattle."

"Danny—" Cameron turned to the boy and studied his face a second. "Reckon you and Cisco could find your way back to the ranch?"

"And leave you here?" Danny shook his head. "You don't know the country as well as me."

"But when I smell smoke I know what direction it's comin' from," Cameron said quietly.

The boy stared at him like a fool galoot until he smelled it, too, just a faint acrid aroma that burning mesquite makes.

"Now can I have a look-see on my own?"

Danny thought to himself, No, sir, this is our range and these are our cattle and no newcomer is goin' to tell me what to do. But he said, "Sure," and smiled for Cameron's benefit.

"You waited too long. Now I don't trust you." Cameron shrugged. "We'll all go back together."

"Listen—" Danny was mad because Cameron had read his mind and caught him in a lie. "We can't back off."

"It can wait," Cameron said.

"I have my knife," Cisco said, touching the bone handle of his bowie.

"You really mean you're afraid." Danny said what he'd wanted to say all along.

"We're not going to argue about it," Cameron said, turning his gray homeward. "Let's move out."

By then Danny knew the smoke came from over by the river and he thought, Why should we ride all this way then turn around and go back because of a little smoke?

"Danny—," the big man said firmly.

Danny turned Topsy hard and hit him with the reins, startling him and sending him flying toward the river.

He was lying over Topsy's neck, his chin in the mane, when the rawhide reata dropped over Topsy's head and tightened. Topsy, trained to know that a good horse stopped when he feels the loop around his neck, turned and faced the rope.

On the other end of the reata Cisco dallied out line so as not to hurt the pony, but he didn't let go.

Beside him rode the tall gray man.

Danny expected some hot words from him, but all he got was a look of disappointment.

Cameron told the old man, "Leave the reata on him awhile, Cisco. This child isn't old enough to be trusted yet."

He couldn't have hurt Danny worse with a quirt. The boy had no reply. He tried to swallow and couldn't.

They were near the river, which at that time of the year was shallow and slow going, and acrid mesquite smoke drifted across on the breeze.

"Likely they've heard us," Cameron said.

He led the way directly to the bank, where they could see the other side. Near a couple of old cottonwood trees two men stood in front of a small camp fire, watching and waiting.

Danny recognized Drum Biggers from seeing him in town. He was below average height, but his shoulders looked wide as an ox yoke, and he was broad all the way to the ground. Over a blue chambray shirt, he wore a cowhide vest, hair out. Bigger's face was covered with short stubble. In his right hand he held a Spencer repeater.

Beside him was a large, paunchy man who somehow didn't look like a cowpuncher. A dude, Danny thought, but then he saw the tidy way the dude wore the two six-guns tied down to his heavy thighs.

Behind them a trussed-up beef bellowed. From the size of his horns, he wasn't more than a year old. A third man knelt on the bull's shoulder, carving on his left ear.

"You know them?" Cameron asked quietly.

"Drum Biggers," Cisco replied in the same flat-voiced way. "The fat one is Clete de Spain and the one with the bull is Shorty."

"Afternoon," Cameron called as he touched his hat brim with his right hand.

"What outfit you with?" Biggers called back.

"Lazy H," Cameron replied, and without hesitating, urged the gray horse into the shallow water.

CHAPTER 4

HARDLY HAD CAMERON'S gray got his feet wet than Biggers growled something unintelligible and de Spain moved over a step, blocking the view of the small fire. Shorty hopped away from the trussed-up critter and occupied himself behind de Spain while Biggers strode forward, rifle at the ready, further obscuring the activity around the fire.

Danny and Cisco rode side by side, a step behind Cameron.

Pulling up before the burly rifleman, Cameron nodded and said, "Name's Dave Cameron."

"Drum Biggers. You're a far piece from home—"

"I'm new," Cameron said. "Cisco and the boy are showing me the range."

"You look like a road agent wearing that mask," Biggers said as the heavyset dude left the fire and moved up beside him.

"I could lay abed in a back room until I'm fit to look at, but I'd rather be out in the open, working."

"I've seen the Mex and the boy," Clete de Spain

55

said, sizing up Cameron. "Where's Lance?"

"Likely off lookin' for the bottom of the bottle." Biggers guffawed, then added more seriously, "We're brandin' a stray. Light down if you like."

"Much obliged," Cameron said, and stepped down off the gray, but Cisco and the boy stayed in their saddles, waiting. He moved over to the young bull and noticed the left ear had been more than half cut off.

"My earmark is an under-half-crop, but the damn bull jerked his head when Shorty made his cut." Biggers chuckled, eyeing Cameron closely.

"Somebody shoulda been settin' on his head," de Spain said, nodding.

"Accidents happen," Cameron said. "Your brand will make it right."

"That iron hot yet, Shorty?" Biggers growled at the pint-sized cowboy.

"Just about," he said nervously, chunking the iron back into the coals and shifting his boots against an open canvas tool bag.

"Stand steady, cowboy," Cameron said in a low voice that carried extra weight, and even as he spoke, he was on the move.

In a sudden blur, he leaped over the fire to Shorty's side, reached down behind the startled puncher, and seized the tail of a large timber rattler that had come flowing through the river-bank driftage. Stepping clear, he snapped the heavy gray body high over his shoulder, then whipped it back in a swift arc. As the snake hit the end of the arc, Cameron jerked as if he were cracking a black-snake whip. The sudden pop sent the rattler's head flying off into the brush.

Cameron's movements came so fast that Biggers lunged forward a step, jerking up the rifle, and de Spain swiftly drew his revolvers, reacting instinctively, while the others looked on, spellbound.

"Didn't mean to startle you gents," Cameron murmured, tossing the slick-bellied, twisting body of the rattler off in the underbrush. "I was afraid Shorty might just step back at the wrong time."

"Holy Christ," de Spain said, holstering his six-guns. "A man can get himself killed movin' sudden like that."

"You're fast, stranger," Biggers said, lowering the rifle again. "Thank the man, Shorty."

"Scared the liver and lights outta me," Shorty said shakily, his flinty face losing its original hostility. "Much obliged, mister."

"He was some provoked, but likely he wouldn't have struck at you unless you'd stepped on him," Cameron said. "Need any help with that bull calf?"

"Can you handle his hind legs?" Shorty asked.

Before Biggers or de Spain could protest or volunteer, Cameron slipped the rope off the hind legs of the bull calf. Sitting down, he grasped the top leg in both hands and pulled up and back. Setting his left boot against the other hind leg, he pushed it forward so that the helpless bull's genitalia were exposed.

Opening his jackknife, Shorty put his knee on the bull calf's head and leaned over its body to where he could easily grasp the bull's scrotum with his left hand. Stretching the bag out, he carefully cut the bottom third off.

Digging inside through the blood and serum with his thumb and two fingers, he brought out a pair of glistening testicles the size of guinea hen eggs.

The bull calf bawled from under his knee, but paying no attention, Shorty pulled the testicles farther out with his left hand, stretching their cords to the limit while his knife hand pushed the bleeding scrotum tight against the bull's belly.

With a slash, he cut the cords close to the body and tossed the severed equipage off into the brush.

"That'll do it," Shorty muttered, breathing hard.

"You use any medicine on the wound?" Cameron asked.

"With the price of beef the way it is, it ain't worth it," Biggers growled, shaking his blocky head.

"Suit yourself," Cameron said.

"Might as well slap my brand on him while

you've got him down," Biggers said, and pulling the red-hot Bar B brand from the fire, he strode over to the downed critter and set it on his hip, burning the hide just enough so it would peel but not so much it would make a raw wound for screw worms to breed in.

The stench of burning hair faded away on the breeze, and Cameron said, "Let his forelegs loose and get ready to fan him out of here."

When Shorty obliged by jerking loose the pigging string around the front hocks, Cameron let loose his hold and sprang to his feet in one movement so that he was ready when the angry young steer turned and made a pass at him.

Swatting the charging critter in the face with his hat, Cameron sent him back into the mesquite to rest and heal.

"Nice work," Biggers said begrudgingly. "You aim to stay with the Lazy H permanent?"

"Can't say just now," Cameron said, slapping the dust off his backside. He climbed aboard the gray.

Danny had been watching quietly, waiting for Dave Cameron to say something about the rebuilt cattle trap. Thinking that the soldier had overlooked it, Danny blurted out, "What about our trap back yonder?"

"You talkin' to me, kid?" Biggers growled, turning his blocky head quickly to glare at the boy.

"He means it looks like somebody's been using the Lazy H trap," Cameron put in quietly.

"That's on your side of the river," Biggers said. "I just look out for my side."

"But it's just a short ways," Danny said stubbornly.

"You tellin' me or askin', boy?" Biggers snarled, suddenly belligerent. "I don't like no bigmouthed, bald-faced kid talkin' back at me."

"Wait just a second, Drum," de Spain drawled, squaring off at the mounted trio. "You sayin' we're trappin' cattle on your range?"

"He didn't say that," Cameron said before Danny could speak. "Have you seen any strange riders out this way is what he wants to know."

"We see tracks once in a while, but who makes 'em is anybody's guess," de Spain said. "You losin' cattle?"

"They've not been tallied for so long it's hard to say," Cameron said. "It'll take a roundup to be sure."

"We won't hold a roundup until next fall," Biggers said. "Maybe that brat can learn his manners by then."

"We're workin' on it," Cameron said mildly. "You wouldn't happen to know who owns the Windowpane brand, would you?"

"That's a new one on me," Biggers muttered, and turning to the small cowboy asked, "You know that Windowpane, Shorty?"

"Nope," Shorty said, looking at his boots.

"What's it look like?" de Spain asked.

"Four squares making a big square," Dave said. "Seems like some have drifted from someplace down to the Lazy H. We'd like to send 'em back."

"You know as much as we do," de Spain said, smiling, showing deep dimples in his fat cheeks. "Best wait until the rightful owner turns up."

"I reckon by the time fall rolls around, it'll get itself all sorted out." Cameron nodded.

"I guarantee it." Biggers laughed. "By fall everybody will know what they own and don't own."

"Much obliged, gents," Cameron said, and kneed the gray back toward the river with Danny and Cisco right behind.

Splashing across the shallow stream, Cameron led them through the mesquite toward the home ranch.

"You saw what I saw?" Cisco asked, riding up next to him.

"The branding iron?"

"The handle faced us when we first saw them, but after we crossed over, it was pointing the other way."

"So maybe they bungled the earmark and they switched branding irons," Cameron said. "What does it signify?"

"Means we caught 'em in something shady," Danny burst out. "I knew it!"

61

"The bull calf was on their side of the river. He was their maverick." Cameron shook his head.

"They must've run him over there from our side," Danny said angrily. "Otherwise why did they change irons and earmarks?"

"I don't know, Danny," Cameron said. "I'm more worried about what's goin' to happen between now and fall roundup."

"You didn't see nothing wrong in their tool bag?" Cisco asked.

"Just the usual hammer, pliers, horn auger, pigging strings, and odd clutter."

"That Shorty must've pitched the hot iron into the brush when they saw us coming," Cisco said.

Cameron nodded. "I smelled brush char. Maybe that's what brought out that old rattler."

"If you'd found the iron, they'd have planted all of us," Cisco said.

"Maybe that's why I didn't go scuffing through the brush looking for it."

"How'd you catch that rattler so quick?" Danny demanded.

"You just have to know what you're doing and be quick about it."

"How'd you learn?" the boy persisted, frowning.

"Sometimes in the war we'd be short of rations—"

"You mean you ate rattlers!" Danny exclaimed.

"It's not much different from a tough old rooster."

"We have a saying: Smart hands, eat trout," Cisco said. "But a trout don't bite like a rattler!"

"It's just a trick," the boy grumbled, denying his wonder and envy of the man in gray. "You could've stood up for me instead of backin' down like you did."

"I thought under the circumstances, he was right, Danny."

"He called me a bigmouthed, bald-faced kid!" Danny squawked.

"You could've gotten us all killed with your talkin' instead of listenin'," Cameron said.

"Well, you wouldn't say a damn word about our trap!" Danny said accusingly.

"Did you learn any more by asking than you knew before?"

"No, but I sure let 'em know I was watchin' out for our property."

"That might've been a mistake, too," Cameron said. "We'll have to wait and see."

"Now listen here!" Danny popped off.

"*Callette, hijo, por favor.*" Cisco held up his hand to quiet the boy. "Remember how many times I told you—"

"A closed mouth catches no flies!" Danny burst out angrily. "But a man has to speak up for his rights."

"It's not just speaking up, it's standing up, and there's different ways of doing it," Cameron said slowly. "You weren't standing up for your rights when that bull had you up the mesquite tree, were you?"

"That was different," Danny said sullenly. "That grulla had me at a disadvantage."

"I figured us against three gunmen that way too."

"If you wore a pair of six-guns, we'd have been at least even with 'em."

"It's not to be argued, Danny," Cameron said patiently. "Ifs don't count."

"Grown-ups never understand anything," Danny said morosely, but seeing the ranch house in the distance, he hooted and kicked Topsy into a gallop.

"He's some bronco, no?" Cisco said placidly.

"We all were once," Dave replied.

CHAPTER 5

UNDER THE BRUSH arbor, Elizabeth sorted through black beans, picking out stems and little clods of dirt and an occasional pebble. Cisco stared quietly at the sky, his thoughts somewhere else, and Dave Cameron turned a heavy mug of coffee in his big hands. Danny knelt in the dirt, teasing an ant lion with a straw and worrying about Drum Biggers and his heavy, contemptuous laughter.

"I've never heard of a Windowpane brand," Elizabeth said. "Possibly they've bought out Pat Hare or Drum Biggers and not bothered to let us know."

"We met Biggers"—Cameron shook his head—"and Hare's seventy-one would be over east."

"I guess there's nothing to prevent a person from registering a brand, even if he doesn't have the land to go with it," Elizabeth said.

"None of it makes much sense except this Windowpane outfit is takin' everything it can, including your catch pen."

"Biggers never was much of a neighbor until Harry went off to war," Elizabeth said. "Then

65

he started hanging around like he wanted to help out, but that wasn't exactly what he had in mind. I finally had to tell him to scat."

"Over by the river, he looked like the he-boar in the cabbage patch."

"And Danny?" Elizabeth asked, looking over at him. "Did he behave himself?"

Danny knew he'd been wrong to go against Dave Cameron's orders and he knew his dad would have been disappointed in him, but worse than that, his mama had enough troubles on her mind without him adding on more.

He thought he'd better just stand up and admit he'd been a little forward, when Cameron said, "He's way ahead of his age, ma'am, and if he wasn't scrappy, I wouldn't want him along."

She looked at him steadily, trying to read all the things he wasn't saying, and he looked right back at her with his good eye and his scarred eye, too.

Danny wondered if they were trying to stare each other down. He saw a trace of a smile cross Cisco's dark face and figured they all were ganging up on him.

Then he thought maybe their starin' back and forth didn't have anything to do with him at all.

By the time Danny was set to ask what it was all about, his mama brushed the beans off the table into an enamel pot with the side of her hand, being careful not to lose a one, then she went off to the well, leaving the three of them alone.

"Why didn't you tell her?" Danny asked.

"What I told her was true." Cameron looked over at him. "But we're going to have an understanding from now on about who's boss."

"I don't need a boss," Danny said, feeling fractious all over again.

"I'll tell you just this once. There's something out there on the range that's as dangerous as a blind rattlesnake sheddin' his skin in August, and in this matter, I'm boss. That's all there is to it."

"He's older than you," Cisco said to the boy.

"This is my house," Danny said stubbornly.

"Fine," Cameron said. "You stay here with your mother where you belong."

"I'll go wherever I please," Danny snapped back, rankled at being treated like he was tied to his mama's apron strings.

"His daddy would have whipped his butt for that," Cisco said morosely.

"He's just a green colt," Cameron said. "Some take a lot of patience."

"I broke lots of green colts without even a buck, but this one . . ." Cisco shrugged like it was hopeless.

"You don't have to talk down to me, either," Danny said, mad again.

"We're not talking to you, *hijo*," Cisco said, turning away. "You want to fight the hackamore, go fight it by yourself."

Danny stood on the bench and climbed the

pepper tree to his private platform, where he was the undisputed boss.

It hurt to have Cisco push him away that way, like he was a no-good town kid. Cisco had always been extra careful and patient in explaining things before now.

He resented Cisco comparing him to a mustang colt. Cisco's method of training a green colt was to first fit a hackamore over the colt's head so he'd get used to it in time, then add the *mecate*, a thick rope made of soft mane hair that ran up from the *bolsa*'s knot and went around the colt's neck right behind his head with a throat latch and earpiece so that it served as an effective halter. The leftover *mecate* became a lead rope twenty to twenty-five feet long. On the first day of training, Cisco would tie the young green mustang to a tree limb and leave him alone the rest of the day while the colt pulled and jerked on the *fiador*. By the end of the day, his nose and chin would be a little sore from rubbing against the *bolsa* and his neck would be stiff from pulling against the *fiador*, but usually he'd learn to stop hurting himself and behave, finally understanding that the hackamore was the tool his rider used to tell him what they had to do together.

Even though it looked like the colt was losing his freedom, he was really learning a different way of life where he was useful, and generally he was the better off for it.

The rare colt that never accepted the hackamore was generally traded off to a gypsy horsetrader and he'd end up pulling a plow, or worse.

It rankled Danny's spirit to think that he was boxed in and controlled by grown-ups who didn't seem to care about his ideas or self-respect. They hardly admitted he was even there most times, and only when he spoke up for himself did they pay any attention. Now Cisco was saying he had to fight the hackamore alone, and that meant they weren't going to pay any attention to him at all. They just meant to leave him tied to a tree limb, so to speak, until he gave up and knuckled under.

He could have cried just then because of the hopelessness of his position, but he caught hold and told himself that he was too big and too tough to cry. He wasn't one of those soft town kids that bawled every time he stubbed his toe or his ma wouldn't give him his candy.

He was Dan Hamilton, cowboy, fighter, wild horse rider! Dan Hamilton, rancher, beholden to no man.

From up there he could see their domain and feel like the captain of a ship, steering it straight ahead through storms and pirates, whales and cannibals, sharks and giant things that lived in the deeps, ready to reach up and drag the ship down to the bottom of the sea.

He was the captain. He was king. Here he was brave and undaunted, his sword held high.

Here he was an eagle crouched on the bullhide nest he'd built with no help from any grown-up.

Gently swaying in the breeze, thinking of fables he'd learned about knights and dragons, the drowsiness of the breeze's secret potion came over him and he nodded off.

Awakened by a discordant voice down below, he couldn't at first figure where he was or how he got there until he heard his mama say, "Lance, you've been drinking. You've got to straighten up."

"Straighten up and work like your beloved Harry?" His laugh was humorless. "Look what it got him."

"Don't you dare talk about Harry," Elizabeth said sternly. "He was a good man."

"And I can't measure up to him. That what you think?"

"I don't have to think it," she said. "It's plain as a mud fence."

"It's hopeless." Lance's voice sank into a weak lament. "You just don't know."

"What are you talking about?"

"I'm sorry, sis," he groaned. "Sometimes I think I'm so smart, then someone pulls the rug out from under my feet."

"If you can't handle your liquor, then you ought to leave it alone," she scolded.

"I like to drink!" Lance's spirits revived. "Remember? Daddy used to let me have the tap

70

end from his glass? I used to wait an hour by his chair just for that, because it made me feel so big and smart and happy."

"Daddy had his glass every evening, not the whole bottle," she said. "He was a gentleman."

"And what happened to all his fine manners? Sherman's bummers taught him different, just like I told him."

"He was old-fashioned," she said quietly. "He couldn't change his ways. I wish one of us had been with him."

"You think I should have stayed and fought thirty thousand Yankees single-handed?"

"No," she said. "You have to put it out of your mind. I wish you'd quit worrying it like a dog trying to lick a thorn out of its paw."

Next morning, after he'd washed his face in the enameled basin and poked at his hair some, Danny went in to breakfast. Cisco was already at the table with a cup of coffee while Elizabeth rustled around the iron range, looking in the oven at her corn bread, turning the bacon in the big iron skillet.

"*Buenos días, hijo,*" Cisco said as Danny sat down across from him.

"Morning," Danny replied automatically. "Where's Cameron?"

"*Quién sabe?*" The old vaquero shrugged his shoulders.

"You mean he's gone?" Danny asked, waking up quickly.

"Early." Cisco nodded.

"Why didn't he wait for me?"

"Better to ask him," Cisco said in his old cracked voice, but his eyes were alert and knowing.

Danny knew the answer. Cameron didn't want him along!

"He came in early for coffee and warmed-over biscuits," his mama said, putting a mug of milk in front of him. "He said a growing boy needs his sleep."

"It don't make a nevermind to me," Danny croaked. "Who gives a hoot what he does?"

"Settle down," she said, frowning.

"Maybe you will have time to help peg out a fresh hide?" Cisco asked quietly.

"I don't know," Danny replied, thinking Cisco was no better than Cameron.

"I think you better find time," his mama said, bosslady style.

"Maybe I want to practice my penmanship," Danny came back at her.

"That's good news"—she smiled and ruffled his hair—"but when you're finished, you can help Cisco."

Before Danny could object, the door opened and Lance growled, "What's all the damned noise about?"

"It's nothing," Elizabeth said. "Danny's dis-

72

appointed that Mr. Cameron didn't wait for him."

Lance had that muddy green complexion again and his eyes were dull.

"Where'd he go?"

"He thinks there's something not quite right over toward the river," Elizabeth said.

"I was by there just last week," Lance said, suddenly more alert. "Damn it, why didn't he ask me?"

"Too late," Cisco said, getting up and going outside.

"Now what did he mean by that?" Lance demanded harshly, then put his hand to his head as if he'd bumped it on something.

"You weren't here to ask," Elizabeth said, trying to placate him.

"He could damned well wait!" Lance snarled. "He's not even a hired hand and he's already taking over!"

"Hush now and eat your breakfast. I don't know why everybody's so touchy these days."

"I'm touchy because I don't want some stranger taking over the ranch," Lance said, tasting the coffee.

"Don't stretch it," she said. "He's just trying to locate our cattle."

"Couldn't you just take my word for it?" Lance came back.

"They're not all there," Danny said.

"If they're not one place, they're another,"

73

Lance muttered, losing his anger and looking at the tabletop. "We'll have a roundup in the fall, and you'll see."

"Why not a roundup right away?" Elizabeth asked casually.

"Because it's too hot and there's no need. Spring and fall, that's it."

"It's on my mind to find out whether our cattle are on the range or not."

"You just won't believe me, will you?" Lance lashed out again. "Well, I'm sick of having to work this way. I'm going to fire that Mexican, and I'm going to hire a real man who knows cattle."

"You can't fire Cisco," Elizabeth said firmly, "any more than you can fire me."

"The hell with it then!" Lance flared. "You run the ranch any way you want! I can make more money playing monte and have a lot more fun too!"

"Lance, I want your help, but Cisco has earned his place here. Can't you see that?"

"All I can see is a useless old man who won't take orders. I say tie a can to his tail and give him the boot."

"You could learn from him."

"And he could learn to damn well do what I tell him!" Lance started coughing and couldn't quit. "You see?" he gasped, glaring at his sister. "You see what you do to me?"

"I'm sorry," she said, shaking her head.

"That's not good enough. I'm going to town." He got to his feet and headed for the door.

"Think about having an early roundup, Lance," Elizabeth called after him.

"There won't be any roundup if I have anything to say about it," he snarled over his shoulder.

She watched him go off toward the corral, then came back to the table, her shoulders down, eyes wet, chin trembling.

"I don't know," she whispered. "I just don't understand."

"I can help," Danny said, standing up straight.

"I'm glad of that and thank you, Danny," she said softly, "but oh how I wish your daddy were here, too."

"What would he do?"

"He'd take charge. He'd gather the cattle and get them branded. He'd figure out how to pay Mr. Vibor. Darn it, Danny, I guess I'm just not as strong as I ought to be."

"If you lived on a fancy plantation in Georgia, how come you run off with Dad?" Danny asked.

"I was awfully young, but I knew I'd never be happy with any of the spoiled neighbor boys who didn't want to change things. I wanted something else out of life."

"Was your daddy mad at you for runnin' off?" Danny asked, trying to picture her fighting the hackamore and, with dad's help, breaking free.

"Oh, yes," she whispered, her face stricken by the memory. "They took down my portrait and scratched my name out of the family Bible, and I never heard from Mama or Daddy ever after."

"Don't be sad," Danny said softly.

"I'm sorry for those who pay such an awful price for their righteousness," his mama said, her chin up again.

Toward sunset Lance rode into the yard with another man. The big stranger hung his saddle on the rail next to Lance's like he intended to stay awhile.

Lance walked past Danny like he wasn't there, but the stranger said, "Howdy, cowboy," and gave Danny a cheery smile like he was at least somebody. He was about the same height as Lance, but built heavier. His young-looking face was heavy-boned, with a wedge of brow and a lantern jaw. His eyes were quick and wary, and he carried an Army Colt tied down on his thigh like it'd been there so long he'd forgotten about it.

Danny followed along to the summer kitchen, where Lance introduced the stranger. "This is Lou Chamberlain. My sister, Mrs. Hamilton."

The young puncher took off his hat, revealing wavy yellow hair combed down tidy, and made a little bow.

"I'm honored to meet you, ma'am," he said, his

voice sounding slick as Mississippi mud.

Elizabeth nodded at him, looked into his cat eyes, and suddenly looked away. "Welcome to the Lazy H," she said after a second. "Sit down and have some coffee."

"I've hired Lou to help with the cattle," Lance said.

"We can use all the help we can get," she responded. "The question is, how do we pay for it?"

Danny noticed that Lou Chamberlain was eyeing his mama the way a blacksnake eyes a quail's nest full of eggs, and he felt a shiver run up his backbone.

Lou sat down at the table, where he could see her working at the stove. "Don't worry your pretty head about my wages, ma'am. It'll all work out fine."

Elizabeth stirred flour into the marrowgut stew, and her face was red from bending over the stove. Once in a while she'd look at the stranger, then concentrate on the stew again.

"Mighty nice place you have here, ma'am," Lou said in his muddy drawl. "I like it just fine."

"We're just barely holding on right now," Elizabeth said, not looking up, "but maybe little by little we can get things moving again."

"Did you ever shoot anybody with that gun?" Danny asked him flat out.

"Danny—" Elizabeth said sharply.

"That's all right, ma'am. The young man wants to learn," he said, patting Danny on the shoulder. "The answer is yes, I've shot a few."

"How many?"

"Only four so far." Lou smiled. "But I got started late and I'm still young."

"Four!"

"Not that I ever go lookin' for trouble," Lou said firmly, "not this child. But trouble just follows me around like an old hound dog."

"All in one day?" Danny persisted.

"Danny!" his mama said again, firmer this time.

"No, it took a few months, but they was all in the same town."

"What town?"

"El Paso. Always somebody down that way wants to try his hand, you know." He looked at the boy as if he should have known all about it.

"Sure," Danny said.

"Someday when you're not too busy, I'll show you how," Lou said. " 'Course, it takes some practice."

"I've got plenty of time," Danny said, delighted with the invitation.

"After your schooling," Elizabeth said firmly.

Lance came out with a bottle of white lightning and put it on the table. Danny could tell from his eyes he'd already had a drink on the way out of the house.

"Care for a drink, Lou?" he offered, setting out a couple of glasses.

"I take only one drink at the tail end of the day," Lou replied. "I can't afford a shaky hand."

CHAPTER 6

DAVE CAMERON RODE in just before Elizabeth put supper on the table. He shucked his bullhide chaps at the corral and came over to the brush arbor, weary looking from the slope of his shoulders, and gray as the mourning dove.

Lance grinned and introduced Lou Chamberlain.

Lou didn't get up or offer to shake hands, and they both nodded.

"You're just in time," Elizabeth said, trying to bring some harmony among them. "Sit right down."

She acted glad to see Cameron, although he said nothing or hardly acknowledged she was there.

His eyes passed over the bottle of liquor and the two glasses.

"You been out all day?" Lance asked, a little sour.

"All day."

"Which way'd you ride?"

"East."

"Far as Pat Hare's seventy-one?"

Cameron nodded. "Talked to him."

"Well, goodness gracious, tell us what he had to say, Dave!" Elizabeth came forward with a platter of fried steak.

"Said he was thinking about an early roundup." Cameron took off his hat, showing a streak of white hair running through the dark brown.

"Did you tell him I wanted to wait till fall?" Lance interrupted.

"I mostly listened."

"He's quite a talker, all right." Elizabeth chuckled. "What all else did he say?"

"Said there was too many mavericks around. Said folks might be tempted to start branding early."

Lance commenced one of his coughing fits, got up, and went into the house.

"Something to that," Lou drawled. "Loose cattle on open range that ain't branded belong to anybody that wants 'em, same as coyotes."

"This range isn't that open," Elizabeth said. "It's got natural barriers that separate the ranches, so we generally know whose cattle are whose."

"Lucky you've got good neighbors," Lou said, his cat eyes on her face. "A lady like yourself shouldn't be working so hard."

"Pat Hare's right," Elizabeth said, ignoring Lou's sympathy. "Mr. Biggers and us can help Pat mark and brand his whole seventy-one in less than a week. Then we can do ours to the river,

81

then go on over and do Mr. Biggers's Bar B so there won't be any mistakes or hard feelings among us."

Lance came back, dabbing a bandana to his mouth, and said quickly, "I told you once. We'll damn well wait till fall."

"There's no reason to get so stirred up," Elizabeth said, putting a pot of beans on the table. "According to Dave, Mr. Hare seems to think it's a good-enough notion."

"Beth, I'm not lettin' a drifter rep for me," Lance answered hotly.

A little smile passed over Lou's face.

"If you're talkin' about me, better say it direct." Cameron looked up at Lance.

"Glad to," Lance said. "You're not on the pay-roll and you're not reppin' for me."

"I was reppin' for the lady that owns this ranch," Cameron said, his eyes hard.

"I did something today, Cameron," Lance said bleakly. "I hired a regular normal and entire ranch hand to rep for the Lazy H."

"No, no, Lance," Elizabeth chided him, forcing a smile. "You're forgetting this is my ranch."

"Then tell this grub-liner he's got no business here."

"Let's understand something," Dave Cameron said, his voice grating, his eyes striking sparks. "There's somebody else here that you're not seeing. He used to sit right here at this table. He came here and he built this ranch and he gave me orders to help his family and I mean to obey no matter what you say, because I owe my life to him. Clear?"

Danny hunched his shoulders together, trying to look invisible.

Lance backed up two steps, his mouth half open. Holding back a fit of coughing, he whispered, "You can't bring back the dead."

Elizabeth's face went white as she stared at the tall, mutilated man whose eyes were the only way to judge him.

"I didn't want to," Cameron said flatly, "but I've done it."

"You don't have the authority—," Lance croaked.

"My authority is this empty place right beside me," Cameron muttered, patting the tabletop with his open hand.

"I always figured authority was in the barrel of a gun," Lou drawled, putting on a wide grin.

"There's a million soldier boys just been blasted to hell trying to prove that point," Cameron said.

"But it was finally proved," Lou said.

"No, I don't believe it was. The North outgunned us, but in the winning they lost their own freedom."

"How do you figure?" Lou asked seriously.

"It took a lot of money to pay for those guns," Dave said somberly. "Money's grown to be more important than honor, patriotism, or common decency, and now that it's all over, the bankers are in the saddle."

"That's might highfalutin' talk," Lou drawled, "but it don't slice much bacon."

"Now can we all settle down and eat?" Elizabeth said as Cisco hobbled to the table.

The old vaquero looked around wearily, nodded to Lou Chamberlain, and took a seat next to the huddled, silent Danny.

"Lord, bring us peace and harmony as we partake of thy blessings," Elizabeth said before anybody could spear a steak, then she went back to the stove for the coffeepot.

"Did you see a good many Lazy H cattle over east?" she asked cheerfully, pouring the coffee.

"Some," Cameron replied mildly.

It stayed quiet at the table through supper except for the usual talk of weather and conditions of the grass. Elizabeth then cleared off the table and went inside as the men rolled their smokes or carved toothpicks.

While the mourning dove cooed in the pepper tree, it didn't seem like anyone was going to say a word. They were just going to study the ash on the end of their quirlies or pick their teeth.

"Lou's from El Paso," Danny said to get the ball rolling.

"Easy there, Dan," Lou smiled over at the boy. "Everybody's from someplace."

Cisco stood up and murmured, "*Voy a la cama*," and limped off toward the bunkhouse.

The sun was just starting to set in the west, and Danny wished they'd start talking and forget he was there.

"Have you ever been in El Paso?" Danny asked Dave Cameron to break the silence.

"I've been there," Cameron said, nodding.

"Lately?" Lou asked.

"No, some years back."

"She's a red-hot ringtail roarer now," Lou grinned. "They have a man for breakfast every mornin'."

"What's the big attraction?" Lance asked, interested.

"For you, they've got enough monte dealers to satisfy your heart's desire. For me, they've got ladies by the dozen, every one of 'em pretty as a calf in a flower patch."

"Danny, you better hunt your bunk," Cameron said, just when the boy thought the conversation was getting good.

He'd broken the spell and Danny tried to get it back before it was too late. "Tell us about all your gunfights down there, Lou," the boy said.

"Wasn't nothin' much," Lou drawled. "Seems like every time you look around, somebody wants to shoot with you."

"How many?" Danny urged.

85

"Some other time, son," Lou said quietly. "It's not somethin' you brag about."

"But you were the fastest," Danny declared, wondering why he was so shy about his victories.

"I'm here to say so," Lou shrugged modestly, "but you stay too long in a town like El Paso, you make enemies. I got tired of lookin' over my shoulder all the time."

"Damn it," Lance said explosively, "why can't I do something like that! The only place I ever been is from here to Georgia and there wasn't a damn thing worth seeing on the way."

"You're still alive," Cameron commented.

"You saying I run away from the Yankees, Mr. Dave Cameron or whatever you're called?"

"I'm saying those border towns can dirty a man and gut him out sidewise."

"El Paso didn't do that to you, did it?" Lance grinned slyly.

"It might have, but the war came along." Cameron's tone was so spooky the hair on Danny's neck curled up tight.

"Soon as we sell some cows, I'm goin' to buy a Colt .36 belt model," Danny said, changing the subject.

"Why?" Cameron asked.

"So I can shoot things," the boy said. "Suppose I see a rattlesnake? I'll just haul out my Colt and shoot his head off."

"It's more fair my way," Cameron said.

"Grabbin' him by the tail and snappin' his head off is too risky," Danny said, frowning.

"Nobody ever does that," Lance said, disbelieving.

"I'll show you how sometime. It beats shooting it all to pieces."

"I don't believe in foolin' around with either end of a rattlesnake," Lou said.

"It's good training for making a man move fast," Cameron said.

Nobody could tell whether he was joking or not.

The sun was half down by now and the clouds were lighted up with a purple-red fire when Elizabeth came out and took a seat next to Lance. "I always like this time of day," she said quietly, like she was tired and ready to rest.

"We haven't yet settled the overseer problem, my dear," he said slyly, pouring himself another drink.

"It can wait until tomorrow," she sighed. "You're not yourself tonight, Lance."

Lou chuckled to himself, looking off at the sunset.

"Who's boss? Me or him?" Lance slurred, pointing at himself and then at Dave Cameron.

"Neither one of you," she answered shortly. "You can't push me, Lance. Now get your mind off it."

"Then I'm leaving." He stood up on wobbly legs.

"I don't think so, Lance." Lou Chamberlain had a hard tone buried like an iron anchor in all the Mississippi mud. "Better set."

Lance took a long, bleary look at Cameron, sat down again, and rapped the bottle on the table like a gavel.

"Did you know, my dear sister, that Cameron is not this stranger's name?" Lance said loudly.

Elizabeth's head jerked back like he'd slapped her.

"No, I didn't," she frowned, looking over at Dave Cameron.

"I suggest we start using our heads for a change," Lance purred as if he had all the high cards locked up in his hand.

Cameron's eyes moved slowly back and forth between Elizabeth and Lance.

"Am I right or am I wrong, mister?" Lance asked bluntly.

"I'm still just what you've been looking at lately," Cameron said.

"What is your name?" Elizabeth asked in a small voice.

"My old name is gone with my old self," Cameron said. "It's dead and buried."

"Why'd you change it, Mr. Man with No Face and No Name?" Lance was riding high, rowelling Cameron all he could.

"I changed it because I wanted to change myself. Folks wouldn't let me do that so long as they had a name tag on me. When I went to war, I started over."

"What were you running from?" Lance snickered. "An ugly wife and a batch of wailing kids?"

"I wasn't running," Cameron said quietly. "I was just changing."

"So you could look for a well-to-do widow woman maybe . . ." Lance sneered and took another drink.

"Did you have a family?" Elizabeth asked.

"No, ma'am. I had nobody and still don't."

"What makes you think he is not Dave Cameron?" she asked Lance.

"Beth, I asked around town yesterday when you thought I was off on a terrible binge, and you'd be surprised how many good people put the pieces together after I mentioned an ex-soldier who has a streak of white hair, keeps part of his face covered, and hides a short-barreled Colt with ivory grips.

"You been pokin' around in my saddlebags?" Cameron asked, eyeing Lance coldly.

Danny stared at Cameron, all his doubts resurging.

"Have you got something to be ashamed of?" Elizabeth looked directly into Cameron's eyes.

"It wasn't that way, ma'am," Cameron said. "It was just a question of trying to find a better life."

"He's too modest, Elizabeth," Lance crowed. "Our guest here is none other than the notorious brand inspector, Denver Camden, the butcher of old El Paso."

Elizabeth shook her head. "I never heard of such a person."

"My dear!" Lance chortled, pouring himself another drink, "this man of peace who makes a point of not carrying a gun holds the record for the most killings in one day in El Paso."

"Is that true?" she asked Cameron.

"He's not saying that they were McDaniels brothers and cousins, all anxious to put me under," Cameron said.

"You sluiced the whole family, a total of seven, and the story is they were all asleep and unarmed. Is that right?"

"That's not right. The first two tried to drygulch me in the night. A week later the rest of the clan rode in to get square."

"But you didn't stop with just the McDaniels family. There were lots more after that," Lance said, sneering.

Cameron nodded. "The more I shot, the more wanted a go at me. The only way to stop it was to make a fresh start, with a new name."

"Now, dear sister, you can see why I hired Lou Chamberlain."

Danny understood by then that Lance had brought out Lou to give him an edge over Cameron.

The boy imagined the two of them coming

at each other from each side of the bare front yard, then stopping and waiting for his signal, suddenly dipping forward, clutching at their six-guns, drawing and firing . . .

The vision stopped there. Danny didn't really want either of them to fall down dead.

"If Mr. Cameron's put it behind him, why keep picking at it?" Elizabeth asked. "If my husband trusted him, so do I."

"But you have only this man's word that he even knew Harry. And you can see for yourself he's a liar. I suggest, dear sister, that this gun-fighter be dismissed so we can go on about our business."

Lance's voice sounded tired, his words slurring.

"I can't do that," Elizabeth said softly.

"Listen to me, mister," Cameron said directly to Lance. "It won't make any difference if I go or stay. I'm still going to find out what smells worse than a gut wagon around here."

"You're talking about trespassing now." Lance straightened up a little. "Trespassing is dangerous in Texas."

"He's not leaving until he wants to, Lance," Elizabeth said indignantly. "Now I hope that's settled."

"If it was me, I'd leave if I wasn't wanted," Lou drawled softly.

"Mister, I gave my word to a friend and I intend to keep it," Cameron said.

"You can see we're getting along just fine!" Lance frowned. "You've done what you promised, and now you can start off somewhere fresh. That make sense?"

"It would if it were true." Cameron stood up and moved toward the bunkhouse. "But it's not, and you know it."

"Stand over a ways, Mister Cameron." Lou shifted in his seat. "I always like to keep my back clear."

The sun was a red-hot bar on the horizon and sinking fast. In the yellow light Danny looked around: his uncle Lance, sloppy from so much liquor; his mama close to tears from being ground up between her loyalty and her hospitality; Lou Chamberlain sitting there in such a way he could fire his Colt under the table in a blink of an eye, calm and assured, lazy looking and yet animal strong, an occasional expression of contempt crossing his face, soon hidden. Then there was the man who'd massacred a whole clan of gunmen, maybe five or six years before, a man in a gray mask who'd changed his name and occupation and taken off his gun. He stood there unreadable, big, and unafraid.

Crimson light rouged his gray flannel mask, reflecting off the last of the sun. As he turned away, a chaste twilight stillness came over the land accompanied by the cooing of the mourning dove like a distant church bell calling Vespers.

CHAPTER 7

IN THE TWILIGHT, Dave Cameron stepped through the rails of the corral and stood waiting. The gray horse nickered, left the others, and came over as if hoping for a treat.

"Wastin' your time, gray-horse," Cameron said, fetching a gunnysack off the top rail. He rubbed the gray's withers, working down the shoulder to the knee.

When the dried sweat, dust, and dead hair were rubbed away, Cameron dry-scrubbed his back and barrel until the gray's hide shone like a pearl in the fading light.

Working over his heavy haunch, Cameron murmured to the horse, "I wish I could get myself cleaned up so easy."

The horse stood patiently as Cameron moved over and commenced rubbing down the other side.

"I washed my hands of the killing, but it won't leave me be. . . . We should've rode far west where nobody knows anything about El Paso . . . and we will, too, soon as I square things for Harry's family . . ."

He paused to lift the foreleg and knocked his knuckles against the hard sole of the hoof, making sure the frog was dry and healthy, the heel not bruised or raw from working through the rough terrain, the hoof not grown out too far.

"Comin' here was a big mistake, wasn't it, boy?" Cameron murmured to the gray horse, working with the sack again. The gray horse didn't move as Cameron finished his grooming and slowly moved his hand over the polished neck, thinking how easy it would have been to ride away from this ranch if he hadn't made such a simple promise to his comrade.

". . . Still, I promised, and I reckon that's really all there is to it."

Cameron draped the sack over the rail and crawled out of the corral, leaving the gray horse in the shadows with the stars reflecting off his polished hide like moonlight.

Walking over to the bunkhouse, he paused a moment before the door to look out into the darkness, and like a man carrying a sack of sand on each shoulder, he opened the door and went inside.

Lou hadn't come in yet.

Cisco had lighted a coal-oil lamp on the rough central table where he could see to braid a rawhide quirt. Sometimes using a tine broken off a pitchfork as a tool to make openings under the plaiting strands when other strands were to be run through them, he concentrated on the work and didn't look up.

Cameron glanced at the half-finished quirt and noticed that the width of each hand-cut strand was the same and that each plait was drawn up snug and tight.

"Fine work, Cisco," he said, laying out his blankets on the bunk.

"Keeps me out of trouble," Cisco replied without pausing.

"If that's all there was to it, I'd take up leather-work fulltime," Cameron said wryly, coming back into the lamplight.

"You want to go to bed, I'll quit and turn the lamp out," Cisco said.

"No hurry. I don't sleep too well. Fact is, if I start groanin' in my sleep, throw your boot or something at me."

"Bad dreams?" Cisco pulled a long strand of rawhide through.

"Some."

"The war?"

"The war . . . and before."

"Before?"

"You missed Lance's announcing how I used to be a brand inspector over at El Paso."

"I know El Paso a long time. What happened?"

"It started with Old Man McDaniels and his brother. They had a ranch next to the border where they rebranded stolen Mexican cattle. A

95

couple of them tried dry-gulchin' me. I killed 'em. Then the family came in to settle up. We were all about the same age, but they looked like little kids to me, like they didn't have sense enough to pour pee out of a boot, let alone know how hard it is to kill a man."

"Lots of different stories about that," Cisco said, not looking up. "Some say they were ambushed in cold blood."

"The truth of it was that I was running up and down alleys dodging bullets, trying to get free of 'em."

"They miss?"

"No. I took a ball that busted a rib, and another that punched through my butt," Cameron said heavily, "but they were just kids—damn fool kids! One turned out to be a girl in overalls, wearin' a wool hat! There were so many afterward that wanted my scalp, I changed my name and joined up with Hood."

"And then you went off to war."

"It wasn't much different than El Paso at first, except it was masses of men unknown to each other killing each other any way they could, from sabers to cannon."

"It's over," Cisco said. "Now all you got to do is find the lady's cows."

"You think they're gone?"

"No, I would have heard about a big herd movin' out."

"Where are they then?"

"Only thing could happen is they're still close by but wearin' a different brand."

"We didn't see that many," Cameron countered.

"Maybe they're bunching them up across the river." Cisco shrugged.

"I'm going out early, Cisco," Cameron said, slipping his boots off and lying back in the bunk.

Turning down the lamp wick, Cisco said, "I don't see so good anymore, and if I make a mistake I got to take it all apart and do it all over again."

"I wish I could undo my mistakes like that," Cameron said, closing his eyes.

"If you were a Mexican, you could say '*Dios da panuelo al que no tiene narices.*' God gives the handkerchief to him who has no nose . . ."

. . . The gray autumn hills warted with stands of oaks and dogwood seemed to rise, wave on wave, to a mountainous infinity that blended in with the gray, lowering sky, cold with freezing scud gusting across the slopes through the dawn drizzle. The men slogged through wet ravines and around the hills, making for a distant crest blurred by the chilling rain and the defeated sun slinking behind clouds bunched up like clumps of sodden gray weeds.

Cameron was among them as the foot soldiers

mingled with the cavalry and worked their way up the slippery slopes.

Men slid and fell, cursed monotonously, got to their feet again, bent low to keep their balance, an army of them moving uphill toward the long ridge in the cold, gray morning.

His mount was a blue roan about the same color as the day, the clouds, the scud, the cutting sleet, the tall weeds. His big shoulders churned under his rider's hands, his heavily muscled hindquarters quivered as he drove toward the crest where the hunched-over rider could now see sparks of fire and hear the distant clatter of muskets. He passed by a brass twelve-pounder drawn uphill through the muck by a matched team of horses, their postillions leaning forward over their necks. A wheel caromed off a rock, nearly upsetting the caisson as the team continued to struggle uphill.

He passed by unarmed, barefoot men who had come to fight because they wanted to capture a gun, a pair of boots, and a horse before going back home. He passed by a column of marching men dressed in red-and-white jackets and wearing patent-leather–visored caps decorated with gold braid and egret feathers. He passed by a mob of Cherokee Indians wearing fringed buckskin and carrying tomahawks and old muskets. He passed by a horde of bearded men dressed in linsey woolsey dyed butternut brown, and fur caps with the pelt's tail hanging down the back. He passed cavalrymen in gray flannel, and those with white muslin wrapped around their left arms were his comrades of the Third Texas Cavalry.

Orders were passed along. The cavalrymen separated themselves from the foot soldiers and formed themselves into regular companies without ever pausing in their advance toward the ridge.

The commander rode through their ranks, seeing that they were ready for battle, swearing at the enemy, and repeating, "I want their cannon. I want their blood!" His left sleeve was pinned up over the stub of his wrist. His face was hidden under a red beard big as a strawstack that collected the air's moisture in drops and dribbled them down his tunic. "I want their cannon, I want their blood . . ."

Their red-bearded commander spoke with a courier and put his white gelding into a gallop, leading them toward the far end of the gray ridge where the sparks sputtered through the gloom, brighter and louder as they approached.

Word came that they would turn and drive at the enemy's left flank and, breaking through, dash for his artillery on the next ridge across the valley.

To his right rode a big Texan. His rangy sorrel kept its head high. Its wet hide gleamed like fresh blood.

"Watch yourself, Dave," the big Texan drawled, his stubbled face and smile melting in the rain.

"We're out of room. We got to push 'em back, Harry."

"Cannon and blood, cannon and blood . . ." drowned out Harry's reply that sounded like "or go back home and start all over again . . ." but the speech was garbled in the curses, admonishments, commands, and grunting of horses. A bugle blared, then the Rebel battle cry howled into a terrorizing crescendo as they came around the crest of the ridge and charged across the slope, destroying and driving through the blue-uniformed Germans, fresh off the boat. Astounded Teutonic faces, men running, falling. Blond jackrabbits scattering before the cavalry revolvers.

They'd given up the folly of sabers long before as too awkward to carry and useless against an armed enemy, and in the course of battle had acquired the six-shooting handgun, often carrying three or four of them fully loaded because there was never time to reload once the devil's dance started.

Side by side they rode, roan and sorrel, skimming the wet weeds with their bellies, the German recruits fanning away from them, leaving the field to their savage screams . . . cannon and blood, cannon and blood . . .

In the open, owning for a minute a field

unknown and unwanted, they dashed on across the little valley, almost reaching the creek that drained the high ground. Puffs of smoke rose from the next ridge. Cannonballs landed short, but still came bounding across the swale, knocking down anything they hit.

The distant, unseen artillerymen raised their sights, and the white puffs of smoke warned the riders that the next fusillade was on its way.

This time it was a mixture of solid and explosive balls that tore holes in their formation, and as they leaped the swollen creek, the battery on the hilltop added grape and canister to drive an unholy and devastating scythe of splintered iron and exploding steel balls across their ranks.

The strawstack-bearded commander lifted the stub of his left arm to urge them on when it suddenly disappeared and the upper torso exploded, leaving the broad, blocky head without support and in an instant, the white gelding reared and squalled in pain to meet a twelve-pound iron ball that raggedly ripped its head off and sent it crashing on over backward into the path of the two riders. They reined aside to clear the dead but still struggling commander and horse.

A heavy cloud obscured the sun, then closed an iron lid over the valley where all was dark except for the fiery iron balls arching through the sky and exploding among the advancing horsemen.

A lightning bolt flashed through the darkness

and shells exploded overhead, creating a thunder greater than God's, and in that flash of lightning Dave saw his comrade throw up both hands, saw the welter of blood spray from the back of his body, saw the sorrel's eyes popping out, its yellow teeth bared, its shoulder blown away, then felt the shock of an exploding cannonball, the blue-white flame, the instant darkness, the scream tearing from a throat as he fell off into eternity. "HARRY!"

"Goddammit, stop it!" came a distant voice, angry, disgusted, contemptuous, its harshness discordant with its underlying gumbo sonority.

"Hear me! I said, goddamn it, quit it!"

The hard slap across his face broke him loose from the horror and he opened his eyes to see the shadowed face of Lou Chamberlain, bleak and hateful, his right hand raised for another blow.

"You awake?" Lou growled, seeing Cameron's eyes open, "You go on like this one more time, you're goin' to sleep in the barn, hear? I don't have to listen to your crazy howling!"

"He's soakin' wet," came the liquid voice of Cisco. "Let him alone."

"Other way around. I want him to leave me alone. When I go to bed I want to sleep, not wake up to no goddamn crazy catamount screamin'."

"Sorry . . . ," Cameron said faintly, slowly remembering where he was and why he was here.

"Next time I'm just going to knock you on the head with my gun barrel," Lou snarled.

"He couldn't help it," Cisco protested quietly.

"If he can't help it, he can go someplace else." Lou gritted his teeth and pulled back to his own bunk.

"What was it?" Cisco asked. "Talk about it."

"It's a dream that keeps coming back. It was over in Georgia. We were cold and wet through. We—"

"Who?"

"The Texas Third, what was left of us."

"Harry?"

"Yes, Harry was riding a tall sorrel . . . a canister of grape blew up like lightning striking—"

"Will you knotheads just shut up and let a man sleep?" Lou muttered, taking a deep breath. "I don't want to hear it."

"And you?" Cisco asked quietly, ignoring Lou Chamberlain's irritation.

"A second later, chunks of exploded iron knocked me out of the saddle. That's all. I don't remember—" Cameron shuddered, his voice tight with remembered terror.

"Hell," Lou snorted, "people get shot all the time but they don't go around lookin' for pity by screamin' in the night."

"I'm not looking for anything," Cameron said, trying to put the nightmare away from him.

"You didn't have to go fight, and besides, you

lost," Lou grumbled. "Then you expect folks to pat you on the back when all you did was bring down the carpetbaggers on us."

"There were so many good men," Cameron said, staring at the shadowed ceiling. "They were so brave and we believed any one of us could whip five Yankees."

"Jackasses," Lou said meanly.

"We never even saw the Yankees. They were a mile away serving their cannon. We couldn't whip the cannon . . ."

"And now you don't wear a gun and you couldn't lick snot off your upper lip," Lou Chamberlain muttered, his voice trailing away, breathing deeply.

"*Buenas noches, amigo. Venceremos,*" Cisco said, touching Cameron's shoulder and retreating to his own bunk.

"Thanks, Cisco," Dave whispered, still staring at the ceiling.

Sounds sifting into the boy's ears and the aroma of fresh-made coffee drifting over his bunk had no significance in his dreams of doves and rattlesnakes fighting it out, although he never knew which one won. He was awakened by his mama's whispers as she made a quick breakfast for Cameron by lamplight.

By the time Danny went into the kitchen his mama was sitting at the table with a cup of coffee, working over the list of supplies she'd need to bring back from town.

The old house creaked as the logs shifted ever so slightly, adjusting to the daytime temperature. Looking out the window, Danny could just see the thread of scarlet on the eastern horizon.

"You're up early," he murmured, pulling on his boots.

"Mr. Cameron and Cisco wanted an early start."

"Where'd they go?"

"Checking the cattle."

"What about Lou? Isn't that his job?"

"You'll have to ask Lance. He hired him."

"He don't scare me the way Cameron does. He's a lot more friendly."

"Be careful about sudden judgments, Danny," she said. "People need to be proved out first."

"You against Lou?" he asked, the cobwebs of sleep clearing out of his head.

"No. He looks well-scrubbed, and pert as pecan pie. I reckon women just swoon all over him."

"He's going to show me how to work his six-gun."

"There won't be time," she said, shaking her head. "We've got to do our trading in town. Maybe you can help me churn the butter and gather the eggs."

"Why you looking so peaked?"

"It's hard times, Danny," she sighed, then her jaw firmed. "But we're not giving up."

"Giving up what?"

"The home place," she said shortly, like she was sorry she'd said anything. "Go get yourself scrubbed—we might meet the preacher."

By the time he'd dried off his face with a flour sack, he had put it together that his mama was worried about losing the ranch, even though nobody had ever been foreclosed that he could remember.

Sometimes folks would leave their ranches and pull back into the settlements when the Comanches were raiding, but so far as a bank taking a man's ranch, it just never happened.

There weren't any homesteaders taking up the range because they were Confederates, and the Federals had passed a law in the middle of the war that no Rebs could ever homestead land in the United States. Naturally, if a Texan couldn't homestead, it'd be some risky for somebody from Kansas to come down and try it.

Danny jumped about a foot when a voice behind him said, "Hands up!" and he felt something poking his back.

He turned around and looked up at Lou Chamberlain holding his finger like a gun, grinning.

"If I'd been an Injun, you'd have been dead," he said.

"You come up mighty quiet," Danny said, not thinking it was much of a joke to scare the daylights out of somebody so early in the morning.

"Good lesson for you, Dan." Lou winked and dipped a basin of water out of the barrel. Using the yellow soap Elizabeth made from lye and tallow, he commenced scrubbing his face. As he bent over the basin, Danny saw a bald spot on the crown of his head.

"We goin' to practice with the gun today?" the boy asked.

"Some. I may have to light out after breakfast. You know where that Cameron fellow sneaked off to?"

"I didn't know he was gone," Danny lied for no reason he could think of.

Lou looked Danny straight in the eye. "That so?"

"I reckon," the boy said nervously and scooted inside.

When Lou Chamberlain came inside, he had combed his wavy yellow hair back and his face was ruddy from the wash. He patted Elizabeth on the shoulder like an old friend as he passed by, and said, "Good mornin', Beth. That coffee sure smells good."

She filled his cup and put it on the table in front of him.

"Seems like my crew left without invitin' me along." Lou chuckled, holding the cup with both hands. "I suppose you made 'em breakfast."

"Yes," Elizabeth said. "They left early."

"I don't know why they'd do such a thing. I'm

not mad at anybody . . . yet," he said with a smile.

"They didn't say, but I suppose Mr. Cameron is learning the range."

"He's allowed to do that, is he?" Lou asked, eyeing her up and down when she turned toward him.

"He's a friend of the family," Elizabeth answered, turning back to the stove.

"Man don't have any bonafides. No face, no name, no papers. He could be makin' up the whole thing."

"It doesn't fret me," she said, pushing hot bacon fat over the top of the eggs so as to cook them on both sides.

"Me neither. I'm just tryin' to make sense of the ranch operation." Lou chuckled. "I'm sure glad you're steady."

"It's my job," she said, ladling the bacon and eggs onto a platter.

Lou never quit looking at her, and when she bent over with the platter, he said, "My, you smell sweet as fresh-cut clover."

"Eat your breakfast, Danny," she said to the boy, her face flushed.

Danny sat next to Lou and helped himself to the biscuits while Lou slid a couple of eggs and some bacon onto his plate.

"There you go, pard," he said, grinning at Danny. "You'll be seven foot tall if you eat like this regular."

"With a gun, you don't need to be seven feet tall," Danny said.

"Hear that, Beth!" Lou laughed. "That's my kind of man!" Then he quietened down and said, "I've always wanted to have a good wife and a family on a piece of land I could work for their benefit."

"You've still got plenty of time," Elizabeth said, pouring the bacon fat into a small salt-glazed crock.

"But I never found the right woman." Chamberlain sighed. "Most of 'em nowadays are so flighty all they think about is bows and bangles, feathers and ribbons. I want a partner who'll raise the family while I work at buildin' up the ranch."

"There aren't too many single women out this far west," she said. "You ought to be looking back toward Austin or Fort Houston."

"Even if I was to find one, I still wouldn't have the land." He shook his head sadly.

The answer to Lou's dilemma almost popped out of Danny's mouth, but his mama said, "Drink your milk, Danny."

"I never tasted such flaky biscuits in all my life," Lou said. "They're so fine they just melt right in your mouth."

"I use butter instead of lard," Elizabeth said, then Lance came in, his face the color of rattlesnake belly. Danny reckoned he'd already gone outside and thrown up, because he'd washed his face.

"Looks like the bulldog bit you." Lou grinned up at Lance.

"The grade of liquor in West Texas could stand some improving," Lance growled. "I'm damned if I know why we can't get a barrel of old Kentucky bourbon out here."

"The Yankees done helped themselves to all that," Lou said. "You'll just have to make do with that rectified pig swill that's left over."

"I'm not well," Lance said, wiping the sweat off his pale forehead with his sleeve.

"Ready for breakfast?" Elizabeth asked.

"Not yet. Let me see how the coffee sets first."

"Reckon your poor throbbin' head can stand hearin' the grayback and the greaser lit out before daylight?" Lou asked.

"Now . . . ," Elizabeth protested weakly, and Danny knew why.

She never let him say greaser. It was always Mexican. Anyway, the second worst word was grayback, which meant louse.

Of course, Cameron was dressed all in Confederate gray and wore that gray flannel cloth over his face, so it could be read either way, but from the way he said it, everybody knew what Lou meant.

"Is that right, Beth?" Lance demanded.

"Mr. Cameron and Escudero left quite early,"

110

Elizabeth said coolly, making a point of using Cisco's formal name. "I do admire their enthusiasm for plain work."

"Don't try to be clever, dear," Lance said. "Where'd they go?"

"I have no idea. Mr. Cameron said he wanted to ride our boundaries."

"That could be anywhere," Lance grumbled. "You were supposed to watch him, Chamberlain."

"That jasper moves like a ghost." Lou paused and chuckled. "Maybe he's the ghost of your brother-in-law come back to ha'nt you!"

"I don't need any fool jokes," Lance growled.

"You worry too much, boss," Lou grinned. "Everything's taken care of. I just hope they don't have an accident out there in the *brasada*."

"But we don't know beans from buckshot," Lance said tightly. "There's too many loose ends."

They'd forgotten the boy sitting there quiet as a bug in a hole.

"I'll handle the problem, whatever it is," Lou said harshly, suddenly angry. "You worry too much even when you already know it's settled. Now set and eat."

It was like last night, Lou thought. He tried to be nice and easy, but then Lance would play the fool so he'd have to crack down on him.

Lance sat down obligingly and Elizabeth put a plate in front of him.

"You're both talking a dust cloud," she said quietly.

"What don't you understand, Beth?" Lou drawled, showing his dimples and white teeth.

"I don't understand why Lance sits when you tell him to," she said strongly, looking directly at Lou's wide, smiling face.

"That's easy," he chuckled. "He knows I worry when he gets shaky, so he's considerate of my feelin's. He's a gentleman, even out here, just like you are still a lovely Georgia lady."

Elizabeth didn't answer that. She just piled the dirty dishes in the dishpan and shaved some soap into the water.

"If we're going to town, Danny," she said over her shoulder, "you better start hunting those hens' nests."

The boy rambled outside and on down to the barn where the dominickers scratched in the dust and the big, red-eyed rooster strutted around. He was searching through the dark corners and gathering brown eggs in a tin pail when Lou came across the yard, broad-chested and powerful, even though he slouched along lazylike.

"You about ready to practice, old pard?" He smiled down at the boy.

"Sure, Lou, I'm ready," Danny said, setting the pail of eggs alongside the barn door.

"All right, then," he said, "let's just see how loosened up we are."

Nodding at the pepper tree, he said, "Let's pretend there's an Injun up in that tree wants to lift your scalp—"

Without finishing, his hand whipped down to the walnut butt of the Army .44 and came up straight, pointed on the rise. In that motion, his footing changed and his body came into a crouch, all so fast Danny hardly saw it happen.

"Dead Injun!" He grinned, then picked off the caps from the nipples on the cylinder so it wouldn't fire and handed the revolver over, butt first.

It was heavier than it looked and Danny's arm sagged.

Grabbing the barrel in his left hand, he lifted it up and held steady on the pepper tree.

"Bang! Another dead Injun!"

It was a strange kind of a feeling holding that heavy iron piece which had killed four men. Danny stood a little straighter, feeling big and strong, and aimed over the long barrel at his pepper tree.

"Takes a while to get the heft of it," Lou said. "Like I said, you need to practice."

Undoing the tie around his upper leg and unbuckling the gun belt, he tried to fit it around the boy's waist, but Lou was twice as big around.

"We'll rig up something," he said. "You'll get yourself killed if you don't start young and practice a lot."

Talk like that made Danny swell up with manhood. If anybody came at him, they'd sure be sorry. He'd just blow them off to hell and gone, he would.

With some leather pigging strings and a scrap of rawhide, Lou improvised a holster that he tied to the boy's belt and his thigh so it seemed like the real thing. Of course, the gun barrel was down below his knee, but the weight was reassuring, and they were just talking practice anyway.

"If things work out for me here," Lou said, adjusting the leather strings, "I'm goin' to buy you that .36 Colt, and you'll be the terror of Texas. Now let's see you draw."

Danny tried, and even succeeded in pulling the six-gun free of the leather, but once again he needed two hands to aim.

"You're fast!" Lou smiled and patted the boy's shoulder. "It don't make any difference how you do it, just so you plant your bullet smack in his heart before he can get off a shot."

Danny tried again, and it went a little smoother.

"You're a natural gunfighter!" Lou exclaimed, and Danny felt proud as a tom turkey in the spring. "Use the sights now so you'll know later on. When you don't have time to aim close, then you'll just point and fire."

Danny kept it up until his hands started trembling.

"That's enough for today," Lou Chamberlain

said. "I never seen anybody learn to handle a gun so fast. Why, in another six months or so, you could cut down on about anybody in El Paso."

"Really?" Danny asked, ready to explode with pride.

"Sure! I mean it. Like I said, if all goes well here for me, we'll make us up a gunfighting team that won't back down from anybody."

"What do you mean, goes well?" Danny asked without thinking.

"Say we get the ranch to runnin' right, get the cattle in shape, get your uncle settled down, and maybe then your mama might cotton to me some, you know, so it feels like home to me . . ." Lou smiled and pounded him on the shoulder, man to man.

"Danny!" Elizabeth called from the doorway.

"I hear you!"

"You go on and help your mama, Dan. I hope we'll be workin' together from now on."

Danny felt as if he were about six feet tall and he hated to pick up that bucket of eggs and carry it to the house like a chore boy.

His mama gave him a strange look when he came inside, but she didn't say anything. She cushioned the eggs in a box with ripped-up flour sacks, then went out to the brush arbor, where her cheese rounds dried on cane racks, and packed them in a box.

"Now," she said, "I have to change my dress

115

and then we can go. Suppose you could load the buckboard and see to the team?"

"I reckon." Danny nodded and went off toward the barn.

Lance and Lou Chamberlain were already riding out the front gate, and he wished that he had been able to ride Topsy along with them instead of sitting alongside his mama in a buckboard.

He caught the pair of gentle geldings in the corral easily enough and put them in the stalls, where he could slip on their collars and drag the harness over their backs.

After leading them to the buckboard, he secured their traces, rigged them to the pole, climbed up to the seat, and drove them over to the front of the house.

It took a little doing, but he managed to boost the boxes onto the bed and tie them down with an old reata.

"Ready!" Danny yelled at the door and climbed up to the driver's side, big as a boss man.

His mama came out, wearing a long linen duster over her black town dress, and said, "I'll drive. They might take a notion to run with you."

"This team wouldn't run away from a prairie fire," Danny said, not moving. "I'll drive."

She looked up at him for a long moment, then climbed up alongside him, fussed around with her duster, looked back to see he'd tied down her trade good, then said, "All right, driver, we can go now."

He shook the reins and the team started to walk out the gate.

Danny slapped the reins on their butts and yelled, "Git up!" and they came up to a slow trot which he figured was the best they'd ever do.

He perked up some when they came into the main street of Sur Forks, and he sat up straight on the spring seat, trying to look like a veteran stagecoach driver just coming in from Santa Fe. He saw Lance's brown horse and Lou's buckskin tied in front of the Merry Widow Saloon, and they turned down the alley so they could stop in back of Weissgut's Mercantile.

While his mama was in the store, Danny watered the team, put grain in their nosebags, then tied them to an old pecan tree that gave them some shade.

Rambling over to the dusty main street, Danny took his time examining the various business set side by side with a common boardwalk. Sur Forks, being the only town he'd ever seen, received his full attention, although his inordinate curiosity was curbed by the shyness of a boy who had grown up without brothers and sisters, playmates or schoolmates.

Within him was an indefinable hunger to know everything in the world, to soak in new experiences different from the ranch routine that was so familiar to him that its own unique kind of beauty was mostly overlooked. Dave Cameron's snapping the head off the rattler was a first-time ranch experience for him, but the rest of it was nothing more than ordinary life, plain and simple.

Here in town they did everything different. The storekeepers opened the doors at eight o'clock every morning except Sundays and closed them at dark. They all stopped and had dinner at high noon and reopened at one o'clock. They stopped again at six and took an exact hour for supper.

Although horsemen would ride through vacant lots, taking the shortest way from one place to another, wagons had to stay on the blocked-out streets that made the town geometric with right-angled corners. One aspect of town he tried to figure out was why all the businesses were set up cheek to jowl. Why wasn't the hotel over the hill, the butcher shop down by the river, the saloon off in the cottonwoods?

But that wasn't the way of towns. Towns were blocks of buildings next to each other. Tall or low, shed-roofed or peaked, brick or milled lumber, narrow or broad, they all had high false fronts that made them look a lot more substantial than they really were.

He stopped in front of the barbershop and appeared to be inspecting the red, white, and blue-striped pole in front, but really was sniffing the scents of different toilet waters and talcum powders and observing the skinny barber shaving a gent covered with a sheet. Seeing a pile of hair swept into the corner, he thought it looked too short to braid into anything useful.

The next place was a combination wheelwright, cooperage, and carpenter shop run by an old German who was working on a piece of hickory with a spokeshave. The curls falling away from the shave smelled a lot different than toilet water. It was a different kind of perfume that came from a slow-growing hardwood forest instead of a rose garden. In the next building a short Mexican cobbler mended, made, and sold boots and shoes. Here the air smelled of leather tanned with oak bark, sweet and astringent. The large building on the corner was the Rancher's Hotel, its entryway covered by a worn carpet. The whole place reeked of stale cigar smoke.

Turning onto the side street, he passed a church built of red brick. Not a large building, it gained some character from the cross on top of the belfry, where pigeons nested.

A group of boys and girls gathered in the yard by the steps and as he slowed his pace to watch them out of the corners of his eyes, the bell rang and the pigeons fled from the belfry like a herd of stampeding pinto ponies.

The boys wore clean cotton jeans, and blue chambray or butternut-dyed yellow shirts. Their hair was cut so short they didn't need to comb it and they watched him suspiciously, their voices lowering.

The girls were dressed in flowered calico with white collars, their braids tied with bright ribbon bows. They too eyed him warily and ceased their giggling chatter as he slowly passed by, his shoulders sloped forward, his legs bowed out a little, his heels hitting hard, his step as deliberate as a gunfighter's.

A boy and girl came running from across the street and as they tried to dodge around him, Danny moved the wrong way and collided with the boy.

"Outta my way, knothead!" the boy, a head taller than Danny, yelled and pushed on by to greet the rest of his friends.

The girl glanced at Danny, sized him up in an instant, stuck her nose up in the air, and clamped her lips together righteously, like he smelled of horse sweat and cow manure.

Hurrying along now, he looked over his shoulder at the confident, carefree kids, teasing and laughing, and thought, you don't know nothin' about how to build a tree house, snap the head off a rattler, or draw fast, aim careful, and kill your man. You just think you're so smart— but you don't know nothin' except what you read in a dumb old book. . . .

Still, he reckoned, they had some kind of

special power that he didn't. Like they had plenty of money backing them up, or their education was so superior to his own that he could never catch up and be on equal terms.

It was two different worlds, he decided, downcast and sore.

Their shrieks and giggles ceased as they entered the church doorway, and slowly the pigeons returned to strut and coo on the ramparts of the belfry, telling him to get back to his pepper tree and turtle dove.

Deciding he'd ventured far enough off the main street he turned and caught a whiff of carbolic acid seeping from the doctor's office, then turned the corner where the old Merry Widow Saloon stood directly across from the bank.

Noticing Lance's and Lou's horses loafing patiently at the hitchrail, he hurried along because he didn't want to meet either one of them if they were drinking. He slowed down in front of Maggie's Cafe to inhale the mouthwatering aroma of roasting pork and brown gravy, hot coffee and fresh-baked dried-apple pie.

Thinking about it, he wondered if the town ladies baked bread on Fridays the way his mama did. He hadn't seen a bakery anywhere and decided that maybe the rich ladies bought bread made by the poor ladies.

All those highfalutin' kids in the church school probably ate white bread baked by a poor woman, and their mamas wouldn't even deign to punch down a batch of risen dough.

Reminded of his mama, he figured she'd be finished with her trading and maybe she'd have a penny left over for some lemon drops.

Dodging drays, a couple horsemen, and a buggy, Danny crossed the dirt street to look into the butcher shop, Fanny's Millinery, and Kornbaum's hardware, before crossing the street again to the front door of Weissgut's Mercantile.

Going into the mercantile he felt the gloom of shadowy shelves holding jeans and shirts, cornshellers and coffee grinders, patent medicines and hard candy, dried prunes and salt herring, dill pickles and ranch cheese.

His mama was finishing her business with Mr. Weissgut and didn't look too happy.

"Every week you seem to be a little bit more behind, Miz Hamilton. Maybe soon we get it back to even again, ya?" he said, chewing on his lower lip.

"Just as soon as we gather the cattle, Mr. Weissgut," Elizabeth said, forcing a smile.

"What will you do after you gather the cattle?" he asked, wrinkling his forehead and rubbing his hands on his bloodstained apron.

"Why, we'll sell them, of course."

"But who will buy?" he asked, shaking his bald head.

"We'll cross that bridge when we come to

it." She smiled again and led the boy out to the boardwalk, where she let out a long sigh and said under her breath, "Oh, lordy, preserve me from storekeepers."

"Where are we going?" Danny asked as she stepped down into the dusty street.

"Right over there." She nodded at the two-story brick bank building on the far corner. "If you can learn to drive a team of horses, I reckon you can learn something about the banking business too."

Going up the steps of the bank she stood a little straighter, head high, her needlepoint reticule hanging from her left wrist.

A pasty-faced clerk wearing a green visor stood behind the counter in a cage made of turned walnut spindles. "Ma'am?"

"We're here to see Mr. Vibor," Elizabeth said and kept walking toward a closed oak-paneled door in the back.

She rapped on the door briskly, and when they heard, "Come in," she guided the boy into the office ahead of her.

Banker Joab Vibor sat between two huge oak desks: The rolltop sat against the wall, its pigeon-holes crammed with papers. The other, flat and shiny topped, served as a barrier between him and anybody wanting to talk.

He turned his chair around to face them over the flat desk, got to his feet, bowed a half inch, and said, "Good to see you, Mrs. Hamilton. This your boy?"

"Yes, this is Dan. Shake hands with Mr. Vibor, Dan, and look him straight in the eye when you do."

Danny tried for sure. He put his hand out and felt the soft, cold gut of Vibor's hand and tried to look into his eyes, but they were so busy looking here and there and everywhere, it couldn't be done.

He did learn something right then. If you start off wrong, it's not going to get any better.

"Please take a chair," Vibor said.

He was just a cut above a runt of a man, pigeon-breasted and short-necked. His wizened head reminded Danny of a ball Cisco had once made out of rawhide, wrinkled and scaly. His teeth protruded like a jackrabbit's, and Danny wondered how he ever ate corn on the cob. His little eyes were busy as bees in a honeysuckle vine, and he wore a little fringe of a brown beard like Spanish moss underneath his jaw. About the only thing that seemed normal about him was that his gray suit was clean and pressed.

"Now, Mrs. Hamilton"—he tried to smile but ended up looking like a jackrabbit squinching its eyes together—"what can I do for you?"

"About the note . . . ," Elizabeth said. "I've learned my husband won't be back, so I need to understand what's expected."

"I'm deeply grieved to hear that, Mrs. Hamilton," Vibor said, sucking his teeth. "As for the mortgage on your ranch and chattels, the interest comes due in two weeks."

He looked into a ledger, smacked his lips over his exposed teeth, and said, "The amount will be eleven hundred thirty-nine dollars and twenty-eight cents."

"That's some more than the six hundred you charged me last year."

"It's the way of compound interest applied semiannually." Vibor squinched his eyes together again and nodded agreeably.

"I'm assuming you'll give me credit on cattle then, like before," she said.

"I'm afraid not, Mrs. Hamilton. What with the price of beef, we're losing money every day on those you have already committed. The bank really must have the cash." He tried to sound sad and sorry, but it wasn't in his busy little eyes.

"And if I don't have it?"

"Unfortunately, Mrs. Hamilton," he said in his scratchy, pious voice, "we would have to assume ownership of the ranch—"

"I couldn't let you do that. We have no place to go," Elizabeth said plainly.

"There are always opportunities, Mrs. Hamilton," Vibor said, "or may I call you Elizabeth—?"

"Go on," she said stiffly.

"I have a small house here in town that I could

rent to you for very little. The boy could go to a regular school. You could sew or sell baked goods, doughnuts . . . I'm sure we could make arrangements."

"Arrangements?" she asked.

"Well, you see—," he stammered nervously, his eyes moving about like a jittery sparrow, "you're still a young, strong woman. Mrs. Vibor has been ill for some time, I suppose you've heard . . . Don't get the wrong idea, but I put a lot of value on friendship . . ."

Danny was on his feet at the same time as his mama.

"We'll find the money or we'll walk to California," she said, heading for the door.

CHAPTER 8

AS THEY CAME out of the bank, Danny saw a girl about his own age sitting on the steps. Her greasy dark hair was done up in braids and tied with rags, and she wore a thin cotton dress of flour sacks. Between her bare feet was a splint basket with a rag over the top.

"Doughnuts!" she called out with little hope in her voice. "Home-baked doughnuts!"

"How much are they?" Elizabeth stopped.

"Two for a nickel," the little girl said, standing up.

"We'll take two."

Danny couldn't understand why his mama was acting so foolish. It wasn't dinnertime yet, they'd just found out they were broke, and they didn't know whether the mother of the girl who made the doughnuts was any cleaner than her daughter.

"Mama," Danny said, holding back, "I can get by awhile."

"I want you to get more than a couple doughnuts from this," she said, giving him the doughnuts wrapped in a page from *Harper's Weekly*. "I want you to see what the banker would have us

127

do while he sits in his big white house conniving more misery for the working people."

She was still so mad she was sputtering.

As they went across the street, she said, "It'll be a frosty day down below when I give away all I've got for a leaky roof and you peddling doughnuts on the street!"

She stomped on a little farther and sputtered, "I should have shot him, just plain out shot him down like a yeller dog!"

She was some upset.

"Pissant!" she muttered. "Oh, lordy . . . !"

Then, having gotten most of it out of her system, she laughed at herself, punched Danny's shoulder, and said, "It's nasty moneylenders like Joab Vibor that make honest living a thing of joy!"

Then she settled down and told him what he'd already learned. "Remember, Danny, never let yourself get caught in a banker's trap. It's better to rob his bank than kiss his damn boots."

That was pretty strong medicine coming from her.

"Now, then," she said cheerily, "now that we've crossed that bridge, I'm going down to Fannie's Millinery and buying something silly. I'll meet you at the buckboard in an hour."

"Yes'm," he said, glad that she hadn't made him go along to Fannie's little dress shop, full to running over with ladies' unmentionables.

Danny went on over toward the Merry Widow, avoiding fresh clumps of horse manure, and saw that Lou's and Lance's horses were still standing hipshot in front of the oldest building in town.

A long time ago it had been a log-walled trading post with small narrow windows for fighting off the Comanches. After it changed hands, Tom Fortune covered the logs with milled lumber and added on a four-way roof that came down so far that it made a covered veranda clear around the building. Sometimes Tom Fortune's customers would sip their juleps outside on the veranda in the late afternoon breeze, but this early it was still cool inside and the porchway was empty.

The boy sat on a bench over on the side of the veranda. A sleeping redbone coonhound woke up, lifted its head, and stared at him with sad, red eyes.

The doughnut tasted like it had been fried in rancid tallow and Danny carefully put both doughnuts under the dog's nose. The dog sniffed and stretched his neck as far as he could away from them without having to move his body.

Danny's bench was next to a rifle port, a window with hickory bars instead of glass, designed to hold off the Comanches.

He could hear the men inside talking, their voices drifting out, echoing as if they came from a cave.

Peering in through the bars, he saw Lance

and Lou playing monte, Lou dealing the cards. Standing at the bar, facing Tom Fortune, were two big men whom Danny couldn't identify from their backs.

Tom Fortune had been running the saloon forever. Bald and diminutive, he had a face so pale and cleanly shaved it looked like a winter moon rising up over the bar.

He was a small man, but he kept a short shotgun under the bar and everyone knew he'd used it once to mash up a man, and likely he'd do it again if provoked.

Folks said there was considerable hell-raisin' in there in the night, with painted women and accordion music, but from Danny's bench it looked pretty tame.

The cards were dealt out of a box, and Lance concentrated on each one of them, trying to match up the one he'd picked to win. Lou smiled broadly as he snapped out the cards, as if he were sticking a pin in Lance with each one.

"Damn it, slow down," Lance said bitterly.

"The faster we play the more money you make!" Lou laughed.

Lance was steadily losing, bad luck dogging him like doom.

Old Tom Fortune carried a couple of drinks around and put them on the card table, picked up the empty glasses, and watched the game over Lance's shoulder.

Lance had put the last of his chips on an upturned card and was drumming his fingers on the green felt as Lou dealt and called them out: "There's a late eight, a lady, a loose deuce, big five, ace of clubs, ten of hearts, and what do you know? There's my king of spades . . . !"

As Lance slapped the table with the flat of his hand, Lou raked in the chips and turned the cards over.

"That finishes me," Lance snapped. He got to his feet and Tom Fortune drifted back over behind the bar.

The two big men turned at the sound of Lance's grumbling, and Danny recognized bull-shouldered Drum Biggers and the heavyset Clete de Spain.

An honest cattleman should be spending his days on the range, the boy thought for a fleeting second, but already Lou was saying, "Aw, come on, Lance, one more longhorn won't break you."

"No, I'm done for today."

"What else is there to do?" Lou grinned.

"Not very damned much in this dinky little backwater," Lance said grouchily, lifting his glass. "And I'm damned if I'll work like a slave on my sister's ranch."

"It won't be much longer, couple of weeks maybe . . ." Lou showed his dimples again.

"You shouldn't complain, dude," Drum Biggers

131

growled. "Clete and me are doin' all the work."

Danny couldn't figure out what it all meant, but they quietened down when Joab Vibor came in. He was smaller even than old Tom Fortune and he stood on his toes when he came to the bar and ordered. "Brandy, the best."

Fortune poured, and Vibor tasted it before downing half the glass.

Looking around at the room like a bantam rooster, Vibor said to Lance, "Your sister was just in."

"Why?" Lance frowned.

"Checking the date of her mortgage, she said."

"But that's all straightened out," Lance said. "I hope you didn't tell her. I want it to be a surprise."

"I never reveal business secrets, and I don't discuss them in public places either," Vibor said severely.

"Hell, old Tom won't talk," Clete de Spain said, grinning, " 'cause he knows I'd stick a prickly pear in his mouth if he did."

"You should be getting ready for the drive instead of loafing around this saloon all day," Vibor snapped. "There's work to be done. Men to hire, supplies to be laid by, a remuda gathered."

"I'll get at it Monday." Biggers smiled and made a cross on his chest with his finger. "Cross my heart, Mr. Vibor."

"You refuse to take this seriously, but if something goes wrong . . ." the rabbit-faced banker let the threat hang like a smoking bomb.

"What could go wrong?" Lance glared at Vibor.

"For one thing, Pat Hare wants to have a roundup for the whole Sur basin," Vibor said.

"That would be like poking his finger in a hornet's nest," Lou said, ever smiling.

"It's that stranger's fault. You've got to get rid of him," Vibor said to Lance. Finishing his drink, and with his spine arched and his thin shoulders back, Vibor strutted out the door, pompous as a pouter pigeon.

As they were off on the side veranda, half hidden by latticework, Vibor didn't see the straw-headed boy, the old hound, or the two doughnuts attracting flies.

There wasn't much talk in the saloon after Vibor's last blast, and Danny ambled down the side steps to the boardwalk, wondering what sort of surprise Uncle Lance was planning.

Close to the marshal's office, he saw old Ogden Gant sitting in a bentwood oak chair out in front, the brass star on his left shirt pocket. The big Colt Dragoon hung in its holster from a belt that he kept slung over his shoulder.

Sour as a green sandhill plum, he surveyed the street like he hated it, and when he spit his ambeer, he did it with extra force so you could see he wasn't getting rid of his tobacco juice so much as he wanted to show his disgust for the whole street.

He'd been wounded in the Mexican War and wasn't much good for anything now except to remind everybody there was a vengeful law in the town.

Danny thought, looking at his grizzled horseshoe mustache, that Clete de Spain or Drum Biggers, either one, could handle him with one finger, but so far no one had wanted to try.

The boy was in front of the harness shop when he saw the gray horse and gray rider coming down the street at a slow trot.

A few people glanced up as he rode by, but they looked away quickly enough. They didn't want to be reminded of the war, or of others like Cameron who wore battle scars.

Cameron saw Danny and nodded, but turned the gray to the hitchrail right where Marshal Gant was sitting, and dismounted.

"Marshal," Cameron faced the old man and touched his hat, "I'm looking for some information and I'm wonderin' if you could tell me where to start."

"Who are you?" Marshal Gant growled without even looking up.

"Name's Dave Cameron. I'm staying out at the Lazy H."

"Heard Harry's dead." Marshal Gant spat.

By then Danny had sidled up alongside Cameron out of Gant's spitting range.

"I'd like to know where I can find the registry of brands," Cameron said quietly.

"Hell, there ain't enough brands around here to register." Marshal Gant snorted, like Cameron was crazy to ask such a damn fool question.

"There should be a registry somewhere, a county department, or maybe the Cattlemen's Association," Cameron replied evenly.

"Lookin' for trouble?" Gant finally looked up.

"No, Marshal, just the brand register," Cameron said patiently.

"I heard you was a gunfighter," Gant said.

"I gave it up," Cameron said.

"Lost your nerve, or did you take a ball through your spleen the way I did?"

"Neither one. I just started seeing things different," Cameron said. "Wouldn't someone in town have a list of local brands?"

"How local?" Gant asked.

"Say the Sur River Basin."

"Why d'you want it?" Marshal Gant looked like he was doing his best to make Cameron mad.

"Because I'm new here and I need to know."

"Most troublemakers don't last long in this town."

"I'm happy to know that, Marshal. I hate troublemakers myself," Cameron replied easily.

Danny wondered if he was laughing behind the gray flannel mask.

"Your face ever goin' to heal?"

"I'm hoping that whatever's left of it will," Cameron said easily. "The medico said it couldn't be hurried."

"How would I know if you're wanted, wearin' that thing?"

"I'm afraid it wouldn't help you much if I took it off." Cameron had decided to wait out the crusty old man. "Might even turn your stomach."

"I seen worse on the way to Monterrey."

"That was a hard war, too," Cameron said. "Don't ever seem to be an easy one."

"You give and they take. Now I can't work, where's my pension?"

"I'm on your side, Marshal, but I haven't got all day to find that brand book," Cameron said with a touch of impatience.

"That's your problem, ain't it?"

"Maybe I'd better go on down to the bank and ask," Cameron said, shifting his boots.

"Hold on a minute. It's comin' back to me. There was an official brand book once . . . seems like it was handled by somebody here in town . . ." Marshal Gant wrinkled his forehead, then drawled, "It'd likely be that wishy-washy Bragg Forsythe. He handles ever'thing else in the county."

"Bragg Forsythe."

"He's treasurer, recorder, assessor—hell, I don't know what all. Practices law too."

"Where'd I find him?"

"Upstairs over the bank, but he ain't there. What brand you lookin' for?"

"I'd call it a windowpane. Four boxes making a square."

"Never heard of it." Gant shook his head. "I knew you were a troublemaker all along."

"It could be so new nobody except Forsythe knows about it," Cameron said. "Did you see where he went?"

"Over to the Merry Widow."

"Best I take a look. Thanks."

"Looky here, stranger," Marshal Gant said, "if you get your tail in a crack, don't come cryin' to me."

"I sure won't, Marshal." Cameron moved back down the boardwalk.

"I warned you," Ogden Gant grumbled at his back.

"Mr. Cameron," Danny said, tagging along, "there's some fractious men drinking in there." Danny wanted to warn him that he was walking into a patch of nettles, but he wasn't sure of himself. He didn't think Lance or even Lou would bother much, but Biggers and de Spain were a threat all the time, the way grizzly bears or longhorn *cimarones* were.

137

"I'm just looking for one," Cameron said, striding along, one step to the boy's two.

Going up the steps to the front veranda of the Merry Widow, Cameron eased on through the batwing doors without looking back.

Danny scurried around to where the old red-bone hound lay snoozing. The untouched doughnuts were speckled with flies.

Peeking through the side of the barred window, Danny could see that the four men were standing at the bar, plus another medium-sized dude in a striped suit and shiny boots. His chubby face was clean-shaven, but a mass of curly gray hair waved down to touch his coat collar.

Bragg Forsythe.

Cameron stepped up to the bar, said hello to Lance and Lou, nodded at the burly men at the end of the bar, and spoke directly to the man in the suit.

They were only a few paces away from the window, and the boy could hear them plain as a bogged calf.

"Mr. Forsythe?"

"Yes, sir, I'm Bragg Forsythe, brag spelled with two Gs," Forsythe smiled.

"What the hell you doing?" Lance interrupted.

"I'm talking to this gentleman," Cameron said easily, then turned back to Forsythe. "I'd like to discuss some business at your convenience."

Before Forsythe could answer, Lance was on

him again. "Ranch business? Goddamn it, I told you to stay out of my affairs."

"This is my doing," Cameron said solidly. "I don't know as it concerns you at all."

Biggers and de Spain looked like somebody had just smacked them between the eyes with an ironwood club.

"If we can talk in your office—," Cameron tried again, but Lance was having none of it. A look of terrible fear crossed his face, close to panic, and he grabbed Cameron's arm.

"I'm sick and tired of you pokin' your nose all over my range, stirring up trouble, spooking our neighbors!"

"It's Harry's business," Cameron said. "I'm trying to take care of it peaceable."

Lance let loose, his face pale as Tom Fortune's.

"Sounds like everybody's business to me," Lou said, showing his dimples.

Clete de Spain said, "Don't it beat all how a stranger can try to take over."

"Just a minute, boys," Bragg Forsythe spoke up, "if this man has a legal problem, I'm obligated to give him my help as an officer of the court."

"What court?" Drum Biggers growled. "There ain't been a judge through here since before the war."

"Looks like we're the court," Lou chuckled.

"I'd say wearin' a mask makes him guilty,"

Clete de Spain said with a guffaw. "Let's hang the stumpsucker!"

"Gentlemen," Bragg Forsythe protested, "this gentleman wants to engage my private services—"

"How about funeral services?" Biggers laughed.

"Sir," Forsythe sputtered, his face suddenly damp with a film of sweat, "my office is above the bank—"

"Get out of here," de Spain growled, and Forsythe commenced backing up, his right arm high to emphasize some rhetorical point that was never spoken. He backed through the batwing doors and scampered across the street. As he reached the bank, he paused to get his breath.

"Now what was so important about that business?" Clete de Spain moved closer to Cameron's left side, where Forsythe had been standing.

"Sorry, boys," Cameron said, backing up to keep from being hemmed in from both sides.

"No shooting, by God!" Tom Fortune put the short two-bore on the bar.

"We can't shoot him," Biggers said. "He's too yeller to wear a gun."

"But we can beat him to death, can't we?" de Spain smiled.

"I guess you're all in it together," Cameron said to Lance. "I'm sorry to see that."

"In what?" Lance blustered.

"What are you lookin' for?" Lou asked.

"I don't know yet." Cameron stepped back on the balls of his feet, trying to keep all of them in view, yet he was one against four, and sooner or later one of them would force him to turn his back to the others.

"If you mean to fight, let's get at it," Cameron said levelly, taking another step back as they spread out to left and right.

"You're finished," Lance yelled, prancing forward, punching with his right hand.

Cameron's short left hook was a mile faster and caught Lance just below the ear, sending him crashing back against the bar, where his knees caved in and he slowly toppled to the dirty sawdust.

But his attack had started the *pachanga*, and in that split second when Cameron was moving in on Lance, de Spain came from the other side, swinging his own sledgehammer right hand at Cameron's head.

Cameron saw it coming at the last second and leaned forward; the fist grazed the back of his neck. Instantly he countered with his own right to de Spain's middle and followed through by bulling him around with his shoulder. In another second, he had Clete de Spain's left wrist in his left hand so it almost looked like a waltz, except Cameron hooked his right boot behind de Spain's, tripping him over backward.

Too late, though, because Biggers was on his back, both arms around Cameron's neck, like he wanted to bulldog him.

Lou stayed off to one side, rubbing his hands together, a gunman, not a brawler.

Cameron bent forward, humped his back, and threw Biggers over his shoulder toward the door, but he had to roll on with him to keep from getting his neck broke.

Lance was still dazed, but de Spain came up again and ran forward, booting Cameron in the midsection with all his might. Cameron had to take it, but he grabbed the ankle and twisted, and de Spain went down with a howl of pain.

Cameron let loose as he tumbled out the door to the veranda where he was just getting to his knees when Biggers broke loose and kicked him in the side, driving him toward the steps.

Biggers grinned and, rushing again, caught the rising Cameron on the mask with his doubled-up knee, catapulting Cameron down the steps into the dusty street.

Clete de Spain came out the batwing doors, followed by Lance, who pushed de Spain aside and made a dive at the slow-rising Dave Cameron, only to be swatted aside like a pesky pup.

Danny moved to the front and saw Lou standing at the batwing doors, still smiling, rubbing his hands and watching the show.

The boy ran down the steps two at a time as both of the big men landed on Cameron.

The street filled with bystanders making a ring around the four men on the ground.

From the second step Danny saw Marshal Ogden Gant stand up from his chair, shake his head, and go back inside his office.

Now Lance had Cameron's left arm bent behind his back and Biggers had his right pinned down, so that de Spain could swing at Cameron's head with either hand. He landed a solid left, pivoted, and hammered home a heavy right.

Danny saw blood running down from behind the gray flannel and jumped on de Spain's back, grabbing at his right arm, screaming. The big man grabbed Danny by the shoulder and threw him down into the dirt next to Cameron, whose head drooped down, his battered eyes closed, no longer struggling against Lance and Biggers.

"Now then, let's see what this nigger looks like," de Spain said, laughing, as he reached down and ripped off the bloody flannel mask.

Danny saw it. Everyone saw it for a second. Someone moaned. And de Spain lost his grin.

"Hit the son of a bitch again," Biggers said, and about that time Elizabeth crowded into the ring and set a shiny two-barreled derringer right on the bridge of de Spain's nose.

"Leave him be," she said, her face white, her eyes blazing.

De Spain's eyes crossed, and he backed up. Biggers let loose and followed him into the crowd, while Lance got to his feet, leaving Cameron lying twisted in the dirt, his face an unmasked, raw horror.

Elizabeth put the derringer back in her reticule, fished out a gray watered-silk scarf, and covered Cameron's face.

"Just a minute there, ma'am, this hombre's goin' to jail," Marshal Ogden said, stepping forward.

CHAPTER 9

AS THE STREET cleared, Elizabeth dusted off Danny's backside and looked him over for any serious damage.

"I'm all right," Danny protested. "It's Dave Cameron who's hurt."

"I just don't understand what's going on." She frowned. "Lance is acting wild as a tumbleweed in a twister. The banker wants flesh and blood for his damn mortgage, you're attacking grown men, and your daddy's best friend is locked up in the *calabozo*. It's just a wonder Cisco hasn't showed up ridin' a jackass!"

As Danny stared up at her with thoughtful eyes and set jaw, she was reminded of Harry when he was trying to talk a bucker out of bucking or when a bunch of brush-raised longhorns wanted to go their way instead of his.

He'd just set his jaw and keep on trying, figuring things out without losing his temper and not flying off the handle like she'd been doing so often lately. In the end, he'd settle the bronc down or turn the longhorns, and even then he'd stay serious, like he wanted to memorize how he'd done it so he could do it easier next time.

"Now what are you looking so solemn for?" she asked worriedly. "You look just like your—" She caught herself, "just like a pine tree full of owls."

"They didn't have any reason," Danny said, trying to sort out his jumbled thoughts. "He was plumb peaceable until they crowded him all they could."

"It seems like everyone's doin' the wrong things, with them ganging up on Mr. Cameron, then the marshal marching him off," she said thoughtfully. "Why don't we do something right for a change?"

"If I was a little bigger, I know what I'd do to that Drum Biggers," Danny said.

"No, that's not what I mean," she said. "Come on now, we're going to talk to Doc Newton."

"Whatever for?" Danny asked, following along, but she didn't take time to answer.

Entering the doctor's office after a quick rap on the door, Danny saw her speak to a small man in a gray frock coat who wore a neatly trimmed gray beard and a heavy gold watch chain across his brocaded vest.

"Is it an emergency?" the doctor asked.

"I don't suppose it's life or death," Elizabeth said after she explained that Cameron needed tending, "but there was blood from all over his face."

"But he hasn't asked for my aid," the doctor said carefully.

"Can't I ask?" Elizabeth demanded.

"Then you want it on your bill?" he countered.

"Of course," she answered, exasperated, as if the doctor was slow in the head. "He was my husband's comrade."

"Very well, Mrs. Hamilton, I'll go over and take a look at him," Doctor Newton said. "You know, even doctors have to eat."

"Don't we all," she replied diplomatically and, taking him by the arm, hustled him and his black bag out into the street. She pointed him toward the jail.

"We'll be along in a minute," she called after him.

"Now what?" Danny asked.

"Where's his horse?" Elizabeth asked.

"Over in front of the jail," Danny said. "He stopped there first."

"That's convenient," she said ironically. "What else can we do that's helpful?"

"Take him some lemon drops," Danny said.

"Fine." She dug into her reticule and, finding a nickel, said, "You bring some along. I'm sure he'll appreciate the sentiment."

As Danny scurried off to the mercantile, clutching the coin in his hand, Elizabeth walked slowly up the boardwalk, wondering why Lance was running with the wrong crowd and why he was behaving like a fool rooster with his head cut off.

True enough, he'd been such a little darling, their mother hadn't let him cut his hair till he was fourteen. Their daddy had indulged his son because there was so much wealth and so little work that Lance as a boy had a half dozen blooded horses, a brace of retrievers, the most elegant clothes from France, his own mammy, then his own manservant. They'd given him everything except the judgment to know what was right and what was not.

When the war came close, they still shielded him from the harsh realities of battle by sending him west, probably not understanding that the ranch was in hot, dry country where there were no slaves and little money and each man had to stand on his own.

She kept hoping Lance would adjust to the difficult land and the strong people it created, but it seemed he always chose the easy way out, always trying to cut corners and outsmart the rigorous rules of ranch life.

As she approached the jail she met Doc Newton coming out of the marshal's office door.

"My, that was quick," she exclaimed. "Does that mean he's all right?"

"His facial wounds are severely aggravated," the doctor said, nodding, "but he's suffered no new fractures. The excision of half his left cheekbone some months ago will be a long time in healing completely and will leave a deeper scar than the rest of the facial lacerations."

"Then he'll eventually heal?"

"Eventually," the doctor said. "It's the worst I've ever seen. He'll never be pretty, but he'll have a face."

"That's good news, Doc."

"Incidentally, he said he had a spare mask in his saddlebags. If you're going on in, you can take it to him just as well as I."

As the doctor went on his way, Danny arrived out of breath and asked, "What'd he say?"

"Said he'd be right as rain," Elizabeth said gladly, and went to the gray horse at the hitchrail, unbuckled the left saddlebag, and looked inside.

There was the spare gray mask, but she took a quick breath when she saw the gun belt and holster holding a well-worn short-barreled Colt .44, rechambered to take brass cartridges.

"What is it, Mama?" Danny asked.

"Nothing, son," she said slowly, taking out the flannel mask and buckling the saddlebag closed.

Danny had never been inside a jail before, and he wasn't too anxious to visit this one, but his mama was in no mood for argument.

Hanging up the big, scabbarded Dragoon on a peg behind his desk, Marshal Gant looked like he was set to take a little nap and recover his strength. Seeing Elizabeth and her son coming in, he settled into the chair behind his desk, took off his high-peaked hat, and pretended to look through a batch of old papers, his lips pursed, ready to say no.

"Congratulations, Marshal." Elizabeth gave him a big smile. "I just want to say how much I admire the way you handled that ugly situation in the street."

He looked up at her fresh, innocent face and said suspiciously, "Yes'm."

"You did your duty exactly right. Stopped the fighting and prevented more serious bloodshed. Good work!"

"My job," he grumbled. "Them hotheads think they can run me around, they better think twice."

"That's what I mean. If you hadn't been there, johnny-on-the-spot, they'd have taken the law into their own hands."

"Well, this jasper in the mask, I told him I'd lock him up if he made trouble," Gant said, warming up some.

"It takes a lot of nerve to face half a dozen bullies wanting blood."

"Ma'am, your brother was one of 'em," the marshal said reproachfully.

"I'm worried about that," Elizabeth said. "I wonder if you could tell me why he was mixed up with such a bunch of scalawags?"

"It's been goin' on for some time. If I was his daddy, I'd say he needs more work and less play."

"That's good advice," she said, "but it's not too easy with him being sickly so much."

"Keepin' him out there at the ranch punchin' cows might just cure whatever ails him."

Marshal Gant was not only thawed out, he was warming up to the subject of changing Lance for the better.

"I'm hoping Mr. Cameron will be a good influence on him," Elizabeth continued, "but of course, it's going to take time. Can't rebuild Rome in one day, can we, Marshal?" She smiled again.

"You knowed this Cameron fellow long?" Gant asked.

"He served with Harry," she said simply. "Could I talk to him a minute?"

"Figured he'd been a soldier from the look of his face. Takes a jagged chunk of cannon ball to peel a man's face that way."

Gant climbed to his feet and led the way down the hall.

"Cameron, lady comin' to see you," he called, then looked at Elizabeth and said, "Reckon you won't need me. You just go on down the hall and talk all you want."

"I thank you kindly, Marshal," she said, taking Danny's hand and leading the way.

Cameron sat on the edge of the bunk inside the iron-barred cage. He'd cleaned himself up and wore Elizabeth's gray silk scarf tied over the lower part of his face.

151

When he heard them coming, he got to his feet and, with a hitch in his step, came to the bars.

His gray eyes were alert and searching Elizabeth's.

"I just want to be sure you're all right, Mr. Cameron, and give you this," she said, handing the cloth through the bars.

"I heard what you did, ma'am," Cameron said, "and I won't forget it."

"Oh, lordy," Elizabeth said, laughing, "that's not the first time I stopped a razorback hog like de Spain with my little two-shooter."

"Can you get me out of here?"

"Marshal is set on keeping you the night at least, and maybe it's not such a bad idea. Those men are still in town."

"There's things to do. Somethin' is goin' on out yonder I've got to uncover."

"We've got two weeks," she said. "That's plenty of time to sell a few cattle for the bank."

"Don't be too sure." Cameron shook his head. "Lance knows something. So do Biggers and Lou Chamberlain."

"You sound like they're making a plot against us and the ranch."

"I can't prove it."

"You're talking about my own brother, Mr. Cameron."

"It's a hard sign to read," Cameron said. "If I

could see the brand registry that Bragg Forsythe keeps, it might help."

"That book is open to the public. Why don't I just go over to his office and take a look?"

"I want to know who owns the Windowpane, for starters."

"Is that all?"

"One thing . . . have you heard anything about a cattle broker named Joe McCoy, or maybe agents of his, talkin' to the ranchers hereabouts?"

"No," she said, "I haven't. Now I'm going to see about that brand. . . ." She led Danny back to Marshal Gant's office.

"We'll be back in a few minutes, Marshal. I thank you ever so much for your kindness and courtesy," she said with forced geniality.

Gant stood up, rubbed his turkey-egg skull, and said, "My pleasure, ma'am."

They walked down the boardwalk to the bank, but before they climbed the side stairs to the second story, Danny noticed that most of the horses, including Lance's brown and Lou's buckskin, were gone.

An open door was lettered:

BRAGG FORSYTHE
Attorney at Law
County Assessor   *Tax Collector*
Recorder   *Public Works*

"Seems like he runs most of Uvalde County," Elizabeth said.

It was a big room divided into a couple separate cubicles with separate chairs and desks, as if the lawyer stepped from one job to another just by moving to a different desk.

Drawers hung open, papers were scattered on the floor, an oak filing cabinet had been knocked over.

Elizabeth walked around the littered room, glanced at an occasional paper, and looked through a wooden crate half-full of documents.

"He's gone. Skedaddled," she said to the empty room.

Danny remembered the fear on the lawyer's face when the men had started crowding him.

"My, you're busy today."

A dry voice from behind made Danny jump. He looked around and saw the little pouter pigeon banker staring at his mama.

"We're looking for Mr. Forsythe," she said. "Do you know where he went?"

"I didn't know he was gone." Vibor stepped stiffly into the room and looked over the litter. "From the looks of things, I wouldn't be surprised if he's absconded with public funds."

"You mean he kept the tax proceeds up here?"

"No, that money is on deposit in the bank, but he might have received a large payment from someone. Why else would he leave?"

Danny wanted to say that he probably left because he was scared of the bully boys, but he was learning what Cisco had been trying for a long time to teach him: A closed mouth catches no flies.

"Maybe he knew something . . . ," Elizabeth muttered, shrugging her shoulders.

"What do you mean by that?" Vibor snapped, his shifty eyes sparking.

"It isn't likely anybody paid him anything. People don't have any cash money, just cattle. You know that." She smiled at the banker. "So, it had to be something else."

"I'll get some of the men on his trail," Vibor said.

"Why not turn the whole matter over to Marshal Gant? Let him earn his money," Elizabeth suggested.

"He's incompetent," Vibor growled. "He won't take orders."

"I'll just speak to him," she said. "Come along, Danny."

"Mrs. Hamilton," Vibor said strongly, "I'd advise you to let responsible men handle the problem."

"But maybe this has something to do with all of us, Mr. Vibor."

"How could it?" he asked, squinching his eyes.

"Who knows just now? First, we must find the man and ask him." She yielded no information to the little rabbit-face and went on back down the stairs.

At the jail, Elizabeth told Marshal Gant of Forsythe's disappearance. Gant nodded, put on his hat, and said, "I'll take a pass by his rooming house in case he took sick, then I'll ask around."

Elizabeth and the boy went on back to Dave Cameron's cell. He stood in the same place as before, facing them.

"Any luck?"

"Mr. Forsythe seems to have left in a hurry. The brand registry wasn't there." She shook her head. "Would that have something to do with your Mr. McCoy?"

"I don't know McCoy," Cameron said, "but I was told that he's been sending agents to Texas, telling the ranchers he'll buy cattle for real money in Kansas next spring."

"You mean he's going to make a market for our wild cattle?" she asked.

"That's the story. I'd like to have it confirmed before I take it too serious."

"You think Mr. Forsythe can confirm it?"

"Maybe not, but that's another reason for me to get out of here."

"Your horse is still at the hitchrail, Mr. Cameron," Danny said.

Cameron nodded.

"The others have gone," the boy added.

He nodded again, and Elizabeth said, "Come on, Danny, we're way late already."

When they went through the empty office, Danny said, "I'll catch up with you."

She nodded and went out, while he streaked for the big iron key ring hanging on the wall behind the marshal's desk. In a second he had delivered the key to Cameron and was out the front door, nearly running over his mama, who'd stopped to look up and down the street.

"Let's go." He let out his breath. "We got to do the chores."

"My, aren't you a regular champion of the chores." She smiled at him and started off toward the alley between the buildings that led to the wagon.

Only when they were out of town and safely on the trail home did Danny start breathing normally again. He'd broken the law, which he had been taught not to do, and he had no excuse for himself.

"I ain't goin' to sell doughnuts on any street corner," Danny said into the silence.

"Don't say 'ain't'," she responded mechanically.

"Why'd Vibor talk like that?" he persisted.

"I wish I knew. He seems to think we're already broke to his harness and set to pull his wagon."

"We owe him a bunch of cows?"

"Enough to make some difference in the

increase," she said, "but now that we know what's behind us, we can start getting straight with what's ahead."

"I did a bad thing," Danny said, hanging his head.

"Passing Cameron the key?" she asked quietly.

"How'd you know!" Danny sat straight up again.

"I figured if you didn't, I would. I'm inclined toward freedom," his mama said to his great relief.

"His face looked awful bad when he was laying there," Danny said.

"No wonder he wears a mask," she said. "But, you know, the second time I looked, I thought it could heal, like Doc said, and with a beard combed down over it, he might just look near handsome someday."

"Beard won't grow on a scar," Danny disagreed.

"Looked to me to be enough regular skin left," she mused. "Guess we'll have to just wait and see."

They came into the ranch about dark, where Cisco waited for them. A lamp was lighted in the kitchen, but he sat in the twilight on the bench under the pepper tree.

Danny carried in the bag of supplies while his mama hurried with her bucket down to the barn, where the two milk cows were mooing anxiously.

Cisco didn't say anything until Danny had finished; he just sat there leaning on his walking stick with both hands.

When Danny lighted a lantern and brought it out to the brush arbor, he saw that Cisco's left eye was closed, his lower lip split and swollen.

"What happened!"

Cisco set his jaw and shook his head slowly, looking straight ahead.

When Elizabeth came up from the springhouse, she saw the same thing and asked the same question.

"Lance, Chamberlain, Biggers, and de Spain," Cisco said softly. "Lance didn't do nothing."

"But why?" she asked.

"First, there was somebody else. A man in a hurry wearing a fancy suit. Saddlebags full of papers. Said he wanted to show you a book. I gave him a drink of water and made some sandwiches. *Se fue.*"

"How long was he gone before the others came?"

"Maybe an hour. They wanted to know where that man was. I didn't know, so they get mad. Lance didn't do nothing," he repeated, trying to make Elizabeth feel better.

"How long was the man here?" Danny asked.

"Not very long. I went in and got him some bread and meat and a dipper of water. Maybe five minutes."

"They thought he was hiding out here?" Elizabeth stood up.

"Yes. Lance looked, and said he wasn't here."

"Why didn't they just track him?" Danny put in.

"They did after they got settled down. They ain't much smarter'n a dead burro."

"It all started in town," Elizabeth said. "I'm going to give Lance a scolding he won't forget."

"He didn't do nothing!" the old vaquero protested.

"That's what he's going to catch hell for," she said like the bosslady. "He should've stood up to them."

"Mr. Cameron?" Cisco asked.

"Those four beat the piewaddin' out of him," Danny said.

"I seen marks on their faces." Cisco finally smiled.

"He'd like to catch that city dude before the others do," Elizabeth said.

"They probably already got him." Cisco shook his head. "I'm sure glad I'm not him. They wanted that book. They was really mad."

In the morning Danny was just as puzzled as when he had gone to sleep. His head was full of questions and empty of answers.

Cisco came up for breakfast, but he had no more to say. His eye was open and his face looked better, but he was as quiet as an empty cellar. Brooding deep inside, he looked out over the flatland with rheumy old eyes building up a big hate for somebody.

Before noon, when Danny was doing his ciphers, Lance and Lou rode in. Their horses looked like they'd been whipped for being tired out, and though Lou was his usual easygoing, cheerful self, Lance looked in worse shape than his horse.

Lou eased him out of the saddle and helped him to the open door.

Lance had a coughing spell and couldn't talk, but Lou looked at Elizabeth innocently and said, "Good mornin', ma'am. Fine day, isn't it?"

She looked from Lance to Lou and then back at Lance, who was still racked by his cough, then said, "I'll put him to bed."

"Let me, ma'am," Lou said, helping Lance inside. Danny put down his schoolwork and watched his mother pace back and forth until Lou came out again.

"He's got to learn to take better care of himself," Lou said, looking into her angry eyes. "He keeps tryin' to do more than he can do. Seems he wants to prove somethin'."

"He's proving something all right when he stands by and lets you people beat up on an old man!" she snapped, letting her temper loose.

"Wait just a little, Beth," Lou showed his

dimples and put up his hands, palm outward. "It wasn't him or me, and it happened before we knew it. Right away, Lance and me both told those hombres to leave the old greaser alone."

"Then why was he beaten up so badly?"

"That de Spain has fast hands." Lou shrugged. "And I must say how much I admired the way you cooled him off so quick yesterday with your derringer. He turned just pale as a Swede."

"And where have you been since you left here?" she asked.

"Them hombres was bent on findin' lawyer Forsythe. Lance and me tagged along just to make sure they didn't savage him."

"Did you find him?" She was willing to give him the benefit of the doubt because she hoped he was telling the truth. For Lance's sake.

"No." Lou showed his white teeth again, his eyes looking into Elizabeth's. "They lost his trail. I figure he's long gone."

"What was he running from?"

"Likely he stole somethin'. That's why people run." Lou chuckled, and let his cat eyes roam.

"Have you had anything to eat?" she asked, turning away toward the summer kitchen.

"No, ma'am, but I can wait for dinnertime." Lou shook his head and added, "That brother of yours is a hard one to keep on the straight."

"He's going to have to quit his carousing and start working the cattle. We've got debts to pay."

"I reckon Dan and me could round up a few cows," Lou said, turning to the boy and patting his shoulder.

Danny didn't like whatever was going on. On one side, he looked up to Lou, but there was something he couldn't pin down that put a brassy taste in his mouth. Maybe it was the way he was always eyeing his mama, or maybe it was the way his expressionless cat eyes never matched the rest of his face.

Danny abruptly moved away from his patting hand, trying to get his thoughts settled.

He didn't like what had been done to Cisco, even if Lou said he'd tried to stop it. For all his talk, he hadn't shot de Spain or Biggers.

Danny had the image in his mind of Lou massaging his soft hands when the others were beating Cameron down. The boy wanted the easy-going Southerner to be everything he admired, but he was something else. A rider who'd quirt a worn-out horse. A gunfighter who wouldn't pro-tect an old man.

When Danny jerked loose, Lou looked down and grinned. "I know what you're thinkin' about, Dan. You're thinkin' about practicin' awhile with the .44."

The boy didn't answer, because he wasn't sure of anything anymore. He wished he had a dad to say yes, go ahead, or no, go ride your pepper tree, but he didn't.

"Maybe today we can fire for real," Lou drawled, laying on the Mississippi mud.

Danny didn't move.

"What's the matter, Dan? You give up on guns?" Lou laughed again, teasing.

Elizabeth turned from the stove and watched without saying anything.

Danny didn't know what to do. He'd given Cameron the key to the barred door on an impulse, but with Lou, he needed time to think.

Lou had never been anything but friendly. He called him Dan and pard.

"That gun is too big for me," Danny said.

"You know, old pard, I had a hunch you'd say that," Lou chuckled, "and sure enough, you did. Now, just let me go out to my buckskin and loosen my leathers."

He moved smoothly from the summer kitchen into the yard, and Danny's mama said, "Careful."

He nodded, not knowing what he was to be careful about. In a minute, Lou came back with a tied-up flour sack.

"There you go, Dan." Lou smiled and put the bundle in the boy's hands. "She's all yours to have and to hold."

Danny undid the knot with trembling fingers and fished out a box of shells, a black leather gun belt complete with tooled holster, and a blue steel revolver.

Pulling the almost-new lightweight .36 Navy

Colt out of the holster, Danny looked at the fine engraving and inlaid silver. The boy hefted it, aimed down the barrel, saw that it had been rechambered for ready-made cartridges, and said, just to keep from bawling for joy, "It's just right."

CHAPTER 10

WHOEVER THE BELT had belonged to before had put the buckle on the second hole and worn a little crease across it, but there weren't enough holes for the boy's small waist, so they took the holster off and put it on his everyday belt.

Danny didn't dare ask where it had come from.

They walked past the barn and down by the slough, where there were still some stumps and trash left over from when his dad built the house.

Lou set an old pottery ink bottle on one of the stumps and showed him how to set the bottle right on top of the front sight, then set that right at the bottom of the rear sight's notch. Danny tried it a few times until it came natural. Lift and put those three points together, then squeeze the trigger before he thought any more about it.

He dry-fired it several times, thinking it was a lot easier than he'd feared, and already saw himself as a crack shot, Indians and outlaws falling every whichaway, gasping out their final breaths.

"Let's try it with just one round in the cylinder, Dan, so we don't make any mistakes," Lou said, showing Dan how to slip the cartridge into the cylinder. "This way's so quick," Lou said, "I'll have to get mine changed over."

Danny felt honored that he'd been given a better gun that Lou's own, and he lost the misgivings that had been building up in the back of his mind. What better friend could he have than someone who talked to him man-to-man and gave him the best weapon anywhere in Texas?

"You might as well start learnin' the draw while you're learnin' to shoot straight too," Lou said. "But just go through it slow for a while and set your mind on bustin' that ink bottle."

Danny put his left foot forward, then Lou had him move it left so he had a broader base.

"Bend your knees some—it'll shade your time a hair—and make sure your hand hits that butt solid. You don't want to be fumblin' around while somebody is throwin' lead at you."

This was serious talk, and gritting his teeth, Danny practiced the reaching motion until his hand automatically knew the exact distance it would travel to touch the walnut butt and cup it solid.

"Now, go through the whole operation and fire," Lou said. "Go!"

Without hurrying, Danny dropped his hand to the six-gun, pulled it clear of the holster, arced the barrel up while cocking the hammer with his thumb. When the three points came together, he didn't stop to refine it any, but squeezed the trigger.

The ink bottle exploded and he felt the shock of the recoil kick his arm back.

"Perfect shot, Dan!" Lou swatted him on the shoulder. "You're a natural-born gunman, no question about it."

The acrid smell of the smoke, the loud, bucking explosion, the feel of the power in his hand, gave Danny a giant thrill. He forgot that his father lay dead in a nameless Georgia grave, victim of a similar contraption. He forgot the horror of Dave Cameron's face. All of the bad side went out the window in that moment of fire and smoke.

"Let's do it again," Danny said eagerly.

Lou founded a cracked china coffee mug and set it on the stump, but he made Danny back up three steps before blowing it to pieces.

After that, Danny had to back up a step if he hit, or if he missed, stay where he was.

He was a terror with the weapon. In a few minutes he was ready to take on anybody that forgot to say please or thank you.

Remembering the church school in Sur Forks, he envisioned the bigger boy who'd pushed him aside and the other boys, proud and contemptuous in their fancy clothes and wearing nickel-plated pearl-handled pistols, facing him. Then the bigger boy sneering and grating, "You're yellow, knothead," and Danny's hand a blur as it streaked to the pearl-handled butt of his shiny weapon. He would bring it up smoothly as he cocked the hammer, set the big kid's head atop of the front sight, line up the rear, and squeeze the trigger.

The sneering, jeering face disappeared and the china mug scattered in a thousand pieces.

"Nobody calls me yeller," he muttered.

"What's that you say, Danny?" Lou chuckled.

"Nothin'," Danny said, embarrassed that he'd gotten so carried away. "I was just talkin' to myself."

"You're doin' real good, pard," Lou said. "You'll be the talk of Sur Forks before long."

The noise and smoke bothered an old possum that denned under the stump so much he wandered sleepily out into daylight, poking his pink nose into the air blindly, trying to figure which way to go.

"Kill that Injun!" Lou yelled, pointing at the fat, gray little animal moving about in blind confusion. "Blow his guts out!"

In the heat of the moment, Danny drew, aimed, and fired. His bullet sent the animal rolling.

"Hit him again!" Lou yelled.

The possum wasn't moving this time, making the second shot easy.

"Again! Don't let him get away!"

The third bullet smashed most of the small head into particles of bone and tissue.

Danny holstered the Colt and went over to the

bloody carcass and prodded it with the toe of his boot. A chunk of the skull with one eye was still attached to the bloody body, but the eye was already opaque and the fur had lost its gloss. Why hadn't that fat old possum put his bunk under some other stump? Why didn't he have enough sense to stay out of harm's way?

Still, it bothered him that it was dead because of his shooting it.

"Leave him lay," Lou said, looking off toward the house. "Somebody's comin'."

"Who?" Danny asked, still thinking about the death of the possum.

"Better cache that gun out of sight."

"Why?"

"Don't why me just now, Dan, just take that thing off and hide it!"

Danny stuffed the gun and holster under a rusted-out dishpan in the brush and said, "I still don't see why."

"Fact is, Dan"—Lou gave the big dimpled smile—"I lost the bill of sale, so we best not show it off for a while."

"You mean it's stolen?" Danny looked up at him in astonishment.

Lou shook his head. "No, I found it where somebody'd lost it, but I didn't waste a lot of time lookin' for that somebody."

"Well, if you found it, that's different," Danny said, relieved.

"For sure, somebody lost it." Lou grinned.

By then they were in the bare-baked front yard, where they could see two horses approaching.

"That's Marshal Gant in the lead," Danny said.

"Maybe you better go in the house, Dan. He's got a dead man on that packhorse," Lou muttered. "Go call your mama."

Danny ran across the yard to the summer kitchen, yelling, "Mama! The marshal's bringing a dead man!"

"Who is it?" she asked quickly, turning.

"Marshal Gant!" Danny said again.

"Not him, the other?"

"I don't know."

"You stay here," she said, and took off her apron. She went outside, with Danny a few steps behind her. Marshal Gant walked his mount into the yard, nodding to Lou standing by the gate and Elizabeth coming forward.

"Mornin', ma'am." Marshall Gant touched his hat. "Sorry to bring trouble to your front door, but I'd like to know if you happened to see this jasper lately."

Danny saw the striped suit, but he kept his mouth shut. Nobody'd asked him.

"Who is it?" Elizabeth asked, not wanting to look.

"Forsythe. The lawyer in town," Gant said. "Somebody caught him over by the river and misused him some before they shot him."

171

"You mean tortured!" Elizabeth exclaimed, taking a step back.

"He come by Saturday afternoon," said Cisco, who'd come over from the bunkhouse, when he heard all the commotion. "I fed him."

"That all?" Marshal Gant asked, eyeing Cisco hard.

"That's all I know, except he was plenty scared."

"The papers he had with him are gone. Know anything about them?"

"No. He wanted to talk to Mister Cameron or the *señora*, but he was afraid to wait. Said he'd ought to go on to Austin."

Danny was surprised that Cisco spoke up. The old man was the one always telling the boy to listen and not talk, but Danny guessed he felt he owed it to the dead man to tell his story.

"How'd you get your face busted up?" Marshal Gant asked the big question.

"Horse kicked me," Cisco said.

Danny was disappointed that Cisco was afraid to talk about Drum Biggers and de Spain.

"Care for a cup of coffee, Marshal?" Elizabeth asked, her sense of hospitality recovering.

"I reckon Forsythe is in no hurry," the marshal said, nodding. He dismounted and tied his gelding to the post. "Seems like lots of strange goin's on in the past few days, what with that Dave Cameron breaking jail, and this lawyer feller gettin' run down like a rabbit, then a man been around horses for over sixty years gettin' kicked in the face by one . . ."

"How'd Cameron break jail, Marshal?" Lou Chamberlain asked sharply, losing his boggy drawl.

"Some do-gooder passed him the key likely," Gant said, looking at Elizabeth.

Elizabeth led the way over to the brush arbor and went to fetch the coffee.

"How come you ain't out lookin' for him, 'stead of lookin' for a lawyer?" Lou persisted. "That man's a menace."

"Menace to whom?" Gant asked directly.

"He's one of them war-crazy killers. He oughta be shot on sight."

"About all I got to go on is that Cameron had business with the county recorder. They had words in Tom Fortune's place, then both of 'em disappeared."

"Looks pretty open-and-shut then," Lou drawled, taking a seat at the big table. "Hang Cameron and justice will be done."

"Joab Vibor's mighty upset about all the records bein' gone," Marshal Gant said. "Of course, a banker always treasures records, while folks like us do well enough with a handshake to bind a deal."

Lance came out of the house, tucking his shirt-tail in. He glanced over at the dead man, then turned quickly away. Elizabeth poured him a cup of coffee.

"Terrible," he said, staring into the cup.

"You see him Saturday?" The marshal looked up and studied Lance's face.

"In the Merry Widow, when Cameron was talking to him. Not after that."

"You been doin' business with him, payin' taxes, recordin' papers?"

"No, sir." Lance shook his head as if he was trying to keep his teeth from chattering. "Can't help you."

A minute went by with nobody saying anything, then Lance said quickly, "I'm sorry it happened, though."

"It ain't so bad a man dies, but I don't hold with puttin' a red-hot iron on him first."

Lance jerked and spilled coffee. "I didn't know . . . why would somebody do that?"

"They wanted somethin' he wanted to give to your sister, I figure."

"They?"

"Dave Cameron," Lou said sharply. "He did it."

"Was more than one man's tracks." Marshal Gant shook his head, got to his feet, touched his hat to Elizabeth, and walked stiffly toward the gate.

Before he mounted his horse, he stopped and looked at Elizabeth, Lance, and Lou. "There's

174

cattle with a Windowpane brand on 'em over that way. You know that brand?"

"I don't know whose it is," Elizabeth said, frowning.

"Me neither." Marshal Gant mounted up, looked at Cisco, and said, "Be careful of them fractious horses," and led the packhorse with its grisly burden down the trail toward town

"That old fox knows something!" Lance stammered, staring at Lou.

"Steady on, old friend." Lou smiled, calming Lance with his gumbo dialect. "It don't do no good borrowin' trouble."

Lance stared at him a second longer, straightened up, and nodded. "Well, I hope whoever tortured the poor man got what they wanted."

The breeze sighed through the big old pepper tree, and down in the barn a hen started clucking wildly, proudly announcing to the world that she'd succeeded in laying an egg.

Cisco gimped over to the corral and Lou drifted off toward the bunkhouse, leaving Elizabeth and Lance at the table and Danny still standing under the arbor, trying to absorb the conflicting tensions.

One was torture. Nobody except Injuns tortured people, Danny thought. Surely not even the likes of Clete de Spain or Drum Biggers could do such a thing. But Cisco had been beaten by them and the pair had been trailing Forsythe.

It didn't add up.

"Lance—" Elizabeth said, trying to see into her brother's eyes.

"Honest," he gritted out, "I . . ."

He couldn't finish. He seemed to strangle on the next word, then walked in a jittery circle around the table and tried again. "I never . . ."

Elizabeth tried to hold her eyes to his, but he kept up his nervous pacing, his head bent like he was studying hard, trying to figure out how to explain something he didn't want to.

"Tell me," she said softly.

"Honest—" he choked out, and started all over again, "I thought—"

"What?" she asked, more coaxing than demanding.

"Really, I had . . . no idea . . . that . . ." He coughed a couple of times, put the back of his trembling hand over his mouth, still pacing a blind circle.

"No," he said, talking to himself, "he wouldn't . . ."

"Who wouldn't? Tell me!" Elizabeth said a little more strongly.

"Oh, nobody! I'm just jabbering—"

"It must be pretty serious," she said, trying to lead him back to the subject.

"No, it's all going to—"

"Work out for the best?"

"Exactly. Exactly right." He nodded his

head vigorously, still looking at the ground, pacing around and around. "You'll be surprised—"

"I'm some surprised right now," she said, her voice gradually hardening. "How can I run this ranch if I don't know what's going on?"

"That's it," Lance said thoughtfully, "that's exactly it."

"Lance, you're not making sense." Elizabeth kept her temper down. "Why not get it off your chest?"

"I wish . . . well, wishes won't wash . . ." He shook his head, still arguing with himself.

"Lance, you used to trust me . . ."

"I'll work it out." He nodded, then looked at her for an instant and said, "I'll work it out some way."

"Work what out?" Elizabeth cried out, and hit the table with her fist.

"Uh . . . the . . . problem . . ." he stuttered in the face of her anger.

"Let me help, Lance."

"That's the problem." He smiled quickly. "Too much help."

"Listen, if you're mixed up in murder, you're going to need all the help you can get," she said sharply.

"I'm not—no, not me . . . murder, no . . ." He shook his head, reassuring himself. "I'll get right at it. Another week or two and—"

"Another two weeks and I'm going to be up Salt Creek without a paddle," she said.

"Never mind, Beth." Lance stopped and looked at her. "I'll handle it."

"Can I help?" Lou came up so quietly everybody jumped nervously.

"We're just talking about the Forsythe killing," Lance said.

"I figure he must have talked too much and made somebody mad," Lou drawled, glancing at Lance, but settling his cat eyes on Elizabeth. "Lawyers is always talkin' too much."

"Somebody wanted his registry book," she said. "There must be something in it very bad for somebody."

"Or good for somebody else. Likely we'll never know." Lou shrugged. He called Danny and asked, "Ready for more practice, Dan?"

"I want to clean my pistol good, first."

"Good thinking. Take care of your gun, and your gun will take care of you. I'll show you how to break it down."

They left Elizabeth and Lance at the table and went down to the slough, where Danny recovered the small Colt.

"It's a killer, ain't it?" Lou said as they walked back toward the bunkhouse. "I'll tell you a secret, old pard. It don't make a nevermind how heavy your bullet is, if you put it in your man's heart, he's goin' to be ready for plantin'."

In the bunkhouse Lou fetched some oil, a rag, a heavy piece of hooked wire, and a screwdriver, then sat down at the table.

Danny passed him the revolver and Lou laid it right side down on the table. Using the butt of his own Colt, he knocked the barrel wedge to the left, then separated the barrel from the cylinder pin.

Undoing a couple screws, he took the cylinder loose, then wiped everything with the light oil.

"You see how I did that?" Lou asked.

"I think so," Danny nodded.

"A clean gun won't let you down," Lou said, keeping his attention on the cleaning as he drawled along. " 'Reminds me of a time when I was workin' the riverboats and me'n another gambler got in a disagreement. He wasn't a real gambler, though—he was a raftsman that liked to gamble but generally lost. He was also dirty and didn't care who knew it because he was big as a county courthouse.

"He had himself a big Colt Dragoon that took an hour to draw out of its holster, and I had a five-shot Root side-hammer tucked under my arm.

"My Root was a .31 caliber with a smaller ball than this one, but it was still big enough to knock a hole in the front of his skull.

"I picked up his dirty Dragoon and pulled the trigger. The cap popped, but the powder didn't fire. I tried it again, and that one didn't go off either. To make a long story short, every one of the nipples was fouled and not one of his loads went off. I could just as well have kicked him twixt the legs as shot him. . . ."

Danny listened to his slow, melodious voice and felt drawn into the yarn, as if it were himself with the Root five-shooter, cutting down on the giant, dirty raftsman, knocking a hole in his forehead.

"Was that one of the four you shot?" Danny asked, mesmerized and full of wonder that he should have such an older friend.

"No. I never counted him, because he never had a chance." Lou smiled, quickly slipping the oiled pieces back together and at last knocking the wedge over to the right with the butt of his Colt.

Sliding the weapon across to Danny, he said, "From now on, you do it. 'Course, if you forget how, be sure and ask me before you throw it away."

"I wouldn't ever do that!"

"That's a joke, Dan!" Lou laughed. "You're takin' life too serious. Once you learn the gun, you don't need to be so serious."

"Thanks, Lou," Danny said, sliding the shiny revolver into its holster.

"You don't happen to know where that Cameron fellow went, do you?" Lou asked idly.

"No, he didn't say," Danny replied. "Why?"

"I was wonderin' if he'd ever come back is all . . ."

"I think he'll be back all right. He's tryin' to help mama."

"Heck, pard, your mama don't need any more help than she's got, does she? I mean, you and me can take care of whatever she wants."

"I guess so," Danny said, feeling something shrivel up inside him. That manly feeling of being partner to a quickshooting gambler on a riverboat went cold, and he wished he hadn't said anything at all.

"She says 'scat,'" Lou smiled, "boy, we'll sure scat, won't we?"

Danny nodded, not able to force a smile.

"You know, we could help the marshal a lot, too, if we could roust out that fool register book he wants so bad."

Danny didn't remember Marshal Gant saying he wanted the book so bad. He'd said the men who'd tortured Mr. Forsythe must have wanted it awful bad.

"You don't suppose that Cameron skunk is holed up around here, do you, Danny?" Lou asked.

"I haven't seen him," Danny replied, shaking his head.

"Wonder why he'd go so far as to torture a man and then kill him?" Lou asked, eyeing Danny wisely, as if they were partners working on a difficult problem.

"Search me—" Danny shrugged.

"Likely he's a real desperado tryin' to take advantage of your mama," Lou said. "Lucky for you-all I'm here to stop him. Ain't that right, old pard?"

"I reckon," Danny said in a small voice, hypnotized by the mellow, insistent tone and bland eyes.

"You forgot to load your pistol," Lou said suddenly, his smile disappearing.

"That's right—" Danny pulled out the Colt and commenced loading the cylinder with the rimfire cartridges from the extra box of shells.

"Leave out the one under the hammer in case you happen to drop it or somethin'." Lou smiled, getting his good humor back. "I dropped one of these once and accidentally shot a man's eye out. He was so mad he came at me with a pickax."

"What'd you do?" Danny asked, full of wonder again.

"Shot his other eye out." Lou laughed.

CHAPTER 11

AFTER BREAKFAST, DANNY gathered kindling and some blackjack chunks and filled the wood box in the summer kitchen. Then he drew a bucket of water from the well, sprinkled the dirt to keep the dust down, and gave Topsy a scoop of grain. He turned his saddle blanket where it hung on the hitch rail, doing his best to stay out of the house, where he was supposed to be copying out words from his spelling book, words that he knew he'd never use in his whole lifetime, like acumen, bezant, cockalorum, drupaceous . . .

More on his mind was the other book that Cisco had seen in Mr. Forsythe's hands, the local brands' register. Danny went down to the bunkhouse and found Cisco on the bench in front, rubbing tallow and beeswax into his newest reata.

"You're supposed to be studying," the old man said, glancing at Danny with dark, flat eyes.

"I been thinking about what happened when you talked to Mr. Forsythe."

"Wasn't much talk. He was looking for your mama or Mr. Cameron. That's all there was to it."

"You saw the book?"

"Yes, he showed me. It was bigger than your spelling book."

"Did he go in the house with you?"

"No. He wanted to wash his face and drink some water."

"So when you were inside making sandwiches he could have hid the book around here some-place?"

"I guess he could have, I wasn't watching him," Cisco grumbled. "I didn't think he'd steal anything."

"So, it could be around here—or in the barn."

"You find it, somebody will take it away from you."

"Not while I've got my gun," Danny said without thinking.

Cisco shook his old head and muttered, "I hope to live long enough to see you grow up like your daddy."

"What are you onto me about now?"

"You stickin' to the smiley *bribón* like he was family."

"He's treating me better'n anybody else!" Danny retorted.

"You got to learn," Cisco said, slacking the reata and making perfect coils of it. "Sit down on the bench, *hijo*, I want to tell you a story about a jaguar that lived back in the Sangre de Cristo mountains when I was a boy."

"Is it a true story?" Danny asked, sitting down on the bench.

"Yes, I think it is, because my father, who told it to me when I was your age, never lied," Cisco said with a twinkle in his eye as he ran the braided rawhide through his fingers. "This jaguar was a big strong cat with dark spots on his back."

"Was he bigger than a puma?" Danny asked.

"Yes, he was a third bigger than the puma, with a big, wide mouth and eyes like mesquite coals. He lived in a big cave and ate meat, any kind of meat. Quail and sage hens, rabbits and deer, anything he could find, until one day he saw a family of burros grazing in the valley below. He had never seen wild burros before and wondered if they were good to eat. He saw that the burros had no horns and no claws and that their teeth were only good to eat grass, and he thought they couldn't defend themselves from somebody like him.

"He thought maybe their meat tasted bad like an old coon, so nobody would want to eat them, or maybe they had a stink pistol like a skunk. He just couldn't figure it out, but as he was becoming hungrier all the time, he thought it wouldn't hurt to see if he could get a free meal.

"Then he remembered his mama telling him long ago to never fool around with burros because they were very tough animals. He tried to remember if they were dangerous and finally decided she was just trying to scare him so he would eat more rabbits.

"So he went down to the valley and cautiously approached the three burros. 'Don't be afraid,' he said, 'I'm just lonesome because I have no family or friends.'

" 'How can that be?' Papa Burro asked. 'A big, strong, handsome-looking *caballero* like you should have a big family and many *compadres.*'

" 'It is not the way of jaguars,' the jaguar said. 'We always live alone, but I would like to live with you.'

" 'Our house is your house,' Mama Burro said. 'You can come along with us and we'll share with you.'

" 'But I don't eat grass,' the jaguar said, purring, his eyes shining.

" 'You have a problem then,' Papa Burro said. 'You can't eat us because we are tough.'

" 'Would you mind if I just tried to take a little bite?' the jaguar asked slyly.

" 'You can try,' Papa Burro said, 'but take my advice, burros are a lot tougher than jaguars and you'd be better off taking a bite out of a rabbit.'

"But the jaguar wouldn't listen and tried to take a bite out of Papa Burro while Mama and Baby Burro watched.

"Finally the jaguar gave up and said angrily, 'Yes, you are too tough to even take a bite of, but I can swallow the baby burro whole.'

" 'That would not be very friendly,' said Mama Burro, 'and you said you wanted to be friends.'

" 'You are too dumb and worthless to be my friends,' the jaguar said, and swallowed the baby burro down whole without even saying please or thank you.

" 'Burros are too tough for even a jaguar to digest,' Papa Burro said. 'Too bad, now you've outsmarted yourself.'

" 'I feel fine,' the jaguar purred, lying down under a tree for his *siesta*. 'That baby burro is very tasty and must be very nourishing too.' "

"Is that all?" Danny asked, as Cisco paused to take a breath.

"No, of course not." Cisco smiled. "The jaguar woke up and when he did he had a bellyache, and he felt heavy and tired like he had just had a big meal.

" 'See there?' Papa Burro said, 'the baby burro is just like it was and you can do nothing with him.'

" 'A fine kettle of fish,' Mama Burro said angrily."

"Why'd she say that?" Danny asked, frowning.

"I don't know why," Cisco said. "That's the way my papa told me, is all I know."

"Well, what happened then?" Danny asked impatiently.

"The jaguar found a creosote bush and swallowed some, thinking it would make him vomit up the baby burro, only it didn't work, and the baby burro said, 'Send me down more creosote bush, it tastes so good.'

"This worried the jaguar and he went over and ate some bark of the cascara bush, which acts as a laxative, but it didn't work for the jaguar. He squatted behind a bush, grunting and straining to get rid of the baby burro, but it didn't do any good, and the baby burro said, 'Oh, send me some more cascara bark, it's so sweet.'

"By then the jaguar knew he was in deep trouble and ate some locoweed, thinking it would kill the little burro and then he could digest him.

"But, as you know, locoweed don't kill burros, it just drives 'em crazy for a while, and the little burro said, 'Oh, I love that locoweed, it just makes me feel so strong.' And before the jaguar could even belch, the baby burro started kicking as hard as he could, and pretty soon he kicked a hole in the jaguar's belly, hopped out on the ground, and trotted around, kicking up his heels. Then he said to the dying jaguar, 'What's the matter with you, Jaguar?'

"And the jaguar's last words were, 'I should have remembered what Mama told me about burros.' "

"Is that the end of it?" Danny asked. "Are you just trying to tell me to mind Mama?"

"No, no, *hijo*," Cisco said, smiling a little. "I

ask my papa the same question, and he said, 'The story means that if you are going to be friendly with a jaguar, you must be very tough.' "

"And you're saying that Lou—"

"No, no, I'm saying nothing." Cisco shook his head. "Just remember, burros live a long time."

"Maybe you been eatin' that locoweed," Danny teased, then added seriously, "I'll never find that book, listenin' to your yarns."

"That book got a man tortured and killed," Cisco said. "If you find it, better give it to me first thing."

Danny went into the bunkhouse and climbed up on a box so he could see into the eaves, but there was no book among the cobwebs.

The boy rambled over to the springhouse, where his mama kept the cream and eggs and fresh beef. Built next to it was an open platform with a shake roof where Mama churned the butter and made the cheese.

The big cheese press, built by a Mexican carpenter of desert mahogany, stood there, a heavy rock tied to the lever and a tub of cheese slowly being pressed into a five-pound round.

Muttering to himself about Cisco and his jaguar fable, he looked over the drying trays and through the buckets and kettles, but there was no sign of a book.

The blacksmith shop, with its sooty walls, the anvil spiked to an oak stump, and the forge with its rawhide bellows waiting to be fired up didn't seem like the right place to hide anything. Near the door were scrap horseshoes and rusty iron bars. He thought the general griminess would make Forsythe choose a different, cleaner place. That left the chicken coop and the barn.

He headed for the barn first, a clean, sweet-smelling haven that was full of hiding places. It was where loose hens made hidden nests, and bats and barn swallows lived in the eaves.

The wide wagon door was open and Danny stepped inside, wondering just where to start looking. He had taken only a few steps into the soft shadows when he heard a hiss of breath and a thud in a stall toward the back where the shadows were deeper.

"Now!" Lou's voice came strongly from the stall area and Danny moved slowly forward.

It looked like his mama was being swallowed up in Lou's embrace, willing and without resistance, but then she bit his hand.

"Damn you!" he yelped, and slapped her across the face. "Oh, hell," he growled as Elizabeth backed away, "you been pushin' that stuff at me ever since I got here, and then when I want it, you change your mind—"

"You read me wrong, mister," Elizabeth said, gasping for breath. "Now clear out!"

"Clear out? I don't clear out until my boss tells me to."

"I'm still the boss here, and I'm telling you!" Elizabeth said, still breathing hard.

"Why fight it?" Lou recovered his muddy dialect and looked at her appealingly. "Maybe good ol' Lou misread the sign, maybe he was too quick on the draw . . . but heck, I didn't mean you no harm."

"I know what you meant, mister, and I sure do mean what I'm saying."

"If you look at it from my side, you'd understand how honorable my intentions are," Lou said softly. "You need a husband, the boy needs a father, the ranch needs a man. That's the way I see it. If I was too forward, you have my apology."

"I don't give a hoot for your apology. I want you off my ranch right now!" she said with a different kind of anger now.

"Look, Beth, I said I was dumb. I said I was wrong, and I said I'm sorry. Can't you give me another chance, please?"

"I'll give you five minutes to pack your bedroll and git," she said firmly. "You can have your chance someplace else."

Finished with him, she found her split-oak egg basket where it had fallen in the hay, and when she turned to pick it up, he stepped forward, took her upper arm in his right hand, and said in a low voice, "Look, Beth, I really care about you. It's like I've known you from another time

191

when I was a king and you were my queen—"

She tried to jerk away, but he held her arm tightly. Then from the side door came Cisco.

He was a slow, stove-in old man trying to be a swift bullfighter with the big bowie in his right hand.

"¡*Cabrón*!" he rasped. His dark, patient spirit had been pushed too far, and now nothing mattered to him except to stick that knife in Lou's guts.

Lou let go of Elizabeth's arm and palmed the six-gun so quickly he had Cisco covered while he was still five steps away.

As Lou leveled the Colt, Elizabeth swung the basket down on his wrist, and the bullet blasted into the floor.

Without waiting, she turned quickly so that the bowie caught in the oak strips of the basket, and twisted the knife out of the old vaquero's hand.

"Now then . . . ," she said, breathing hard again, "I've had enough of this. You're leaving, and Cisco, *muchas gracias*, is going back to the bunkhouse."

"Are you all right, *señora*?" the old vaquero asked.

"Yes, thank you, but please, let me handle this."

"*Así es*," he muttered and backed away toward the side door.

"I'm glad you did that." Lou smiled, dimples, cat eyes, and all. "I'd hate to have to kill him."

Before she could answer, Lance came trotting through the big double door.

"What is it?" he snapped. "I heard a shot!"

"Mr. Chamberlain's gun discharged and the bullet hit the floor. He's leaving now."

"Leaving? For where?" Lance looked around, befuddled by late sleep and the sudden awakening into a new course of events.

"That's his business," Elizabeth said.

"But why?" Lance asked in a desperate appeal. "I need him!"

"For what?" she snapped. "He seems more like a watchdog than a hired hand."

Lance flinched at her stormy face and turned to Lou. "From now on, you stay away from my sister. You cook your own meals and don't come up to the house. Understand?"

"It won't wash," she said. "I want him clear off the range."

"Sis, I can't fire him now—" Lance protested.

"Why not? He hasn't done a lick of ranch work since he's been here," she said. "You don't need him. I sure don't need him. Say good-bye and good luck."

"You better change her mind," Lou told Lance.

"Elizabeth," Lance pleaded, "I need him. God knows I hate to ask this favor of you, but he's necessary to my plan."

"What plan? Why won't you tell me what's going on?"

"Just give me another week. I promise it'll be the best surprise of your life." He forced a smile and an old-timey heartiness.

"Lance, I love you, but I'm worried too. I keep thinking you're in something way over your head."

"I'm a grown man, my dear," Lance said stiffly. "You must trust me."

"This coyote can stay, on one condition. That is, he hauls his bedroll down by the slough and stays clear of me and my house."

"You can do that, can't you, Lou?" Lance looked pleadingly at the stocky, ever-smiling gunfighter. "It's only for a few days."

"I just want to prove to the lady that I'm as good as anybody else and surely mean her no harm," Lou said, laying on the thick gumbo.

Elizabeth jerked the knife out of her egg basket and went out the big door.

Danny slipped out the side door, and while she went up toward the house, he turned left toward the bunkhouse and found Cisco sitting on the bench in front, staring off at the hot, hagridden horizon.

"You mustn't ever try to fight with a knife against a gun, Cisco," the boy said, trying to find some sympathetic ground they could share.

"*Se hizo miel y se lo comieron las moscos*," Cisco said stolidly. "He turned himself into honey, and he was eaten up by flies."

"He'd have killed you," Danny said.

"For me it don't make no difference," Cisco replied after a while.

"It does to me." Danny put his small hand on top of Cisco's.

"You be careful," Cisco said.

"You, too," the boy said, leaving him and going off toward the house.

Elizabeth sat Danny down at the outside table with pen, ink, and the dog-eared spelling book.

"I want no more interrupting your schoolwork," she said sternly and told him to copy out a row of words, then recopy them until he'd learned them by heart.

Danny commenced writing, but his mind was elsewhere. He was thinking about the smiling man he'd thought was his friend. What was he here for if not to work?

His hen tracks were nearly illegible because he wasn't paying attention, but he had covered both sides of a page when the three men rode into the yard.

"Mama!" Danny yelled.

She came out, brushed her hair back, and recognizing the men, smiled and said, "Pleased to see you, Pat. Light down and have a cup of coffee."

Danny remembered Pat Hare and his son, Kit. The other man was a hired hand who stayed back of the others and kept quiet.

Pat and Kit dismounted, and Danny put his

195

spelling lesson away so the table was clear when they sat down.

"You're looking good, Elizabeth," Pat Hare said, to get started on the right foot.

He was a long-drink-of-water kind of man, the years pulling down his shoulders. His big hat came down to ride on his jug ears, and his fair-skinned face was a rust color from sunburn, but his blue eyes sparkled with the enjoyment of simple day-to-day happenings.

Back from the war, his son, Kit, had the same long, tall body, but his shoulders were still up and he was holding himself in. He had no good humor or pleasure on his hawkish face, rather, a frosty cloud of impatience.

Elizabeth set out the cups and poured the coffee.

"It's been a coon's age, neighbor," she said, smiling, and put out a plate of fresh baked bread she'd already buttered.

"It has, it has," Pat Hare declared. "We all better have us an old-time barbecue over in the pecan grove soon as we can.

"What brings you all the way over here on a hot day, or are you inviting us to the picnic?" she asked, standing next to Danny.

"Nothin' special, Elizabeth," the old rancher said. "It's just, I been some worried about the cattle. You know, we ain't made a roundup for three or four years now."

About then Lance came out, shook hands all around, and sat down next to Kit Hare.

"Pat's interested in us joining up to brand the stock," Elizabeth said.

"In July?" Lance smiled. "It's a little late or a little early."

"I grant you that, Lance." Pat Hare nodded, his voice scratchy from disuse. "But it's been so long and there's so many mavericks out there to tempt the grub-line riders, I been thinkin' it wouldn't hurt to just get at it. We could start with yours first, or mine, it makes no nevermind to me. We could get the Bar B over, too, and make it easier."

"Did you have any particular day in mind?"

"Heck, we could start tomorrow, if you could reach Drum Biggers and his crew."

"That's a little too soon for me," Lance said quickly before Elizabeth could agree. "Any particular reason for the rush?"

"I heard about Bragg Forsythe," Pat Hare said. "That sort of commotion makes me uneasy."

"I'd like at least a week," Lance said.

"We've seen a strange brand on our range," Kit Hare blurted out.

"Yes," Pat Hare nodded calmly, like he hadn't a care in the world. "That, too. And I've got a note at the bank like everybody else. I reckon we'll just go ahead and start rounding up our own mavericks, and you can join up with us whenever you can."

"You mean you want to start without us?" Lance exclaimed. "I always thought everyone worked together."

"We did, and enjoyed it, too," Pat Hare said, getting to his feet, "but as I said, I'm uneasy. Much obliged for your hospitality, Elizabeth."

"We'll all be over tomorrow if we can get things together, Pat," she said. "Say hello to Ada Belle for me."

"I'll do that, Elizabeth. She sends her salutations as well."

The old rancher nodded his head to Elizabeth, touched his hat, and in a minute they were gone.

Off by the springhouse Danny saw Lou Chamberlain backing into the shadows.

"He's not the only one uneasy," Elizabeth said and frowned. "Can you ride over to Biggers's ranch and invite him to share the roundup?"

"Beth, I told you I need a week," Lance said, desperation all over his face.

"Will you ride over the river to Biggers's or do I?" she said flat out.

"I'll send Lou," Lance said, defeated, but he had to add, "I hope you won't be sorry for pushing on me so hard."

"Don't you see?" Elizabeth was exasperated. "Pat Hare said he'd start without us, and we can't be that unneighborly."

"He's just a burrhead cracker," Lance snarled. "A knotheaded damnfool cowboy that don't know a good cigar from coyote scat!"

"He's always friendly and helpful, always honest and aboveboard."

"You saying I'm not?" Lance demanded.

"I'm not sure anymore," she said, turning away to gather up the cups. "I'll be taking the buckboard to town for our share of supplies."

"Talking about being honest and aboveboard— that's not why you're going," Lance sneered.

"Why else?" She turned to face him.

"That raw-faced Cameron. You're hoping he'll be hanging around."

"I sure am," she retorted hotly. "We ought to have at least one man at the roundup, and I doubt you or your watchdog can even pee on a fencepost!"

Elizabeth decided Danny should catch up on his ciphers rather than waste his time riding along to Sur Forks, and as he was settling down to do his tables, Lance saddled up his sorrel. With Lou on his buckskin, the two rode off west toward Biggers's Bar B.

The sun stood overhead and the breeze came from the north, moving the old pepper tree's limbs in a gentle rhythm, and the mourning dove started cooing.

Danny worked through the fours and had started on the fives when it occurred to him that now was the perfect time to look for the brand registry book.

The rest of the ranch was quiet. Cisco lay dozing, down by the bunkhouse. The hens had already laid their eggs and there was nothing left for the rooster worth crowing about.

Danny tried again to put himself in Forsythe's place. He'd ridden in hot and tired. He'd talked to Cisco, wanting Mama to see the book, but then changed his mind by the time Cisco had come out with the sandwiches.

He'd had a dipper of water and ridden on toward the Austin trail.

Why hadn't he waited?

Still, his killers had tortured him because he didn't have the book, and that just meant the lawyer had to have hidden it here on the ranch. Somewhere right here under Danny's nose.

The boy went back down to the barn and searched high and low, but only came up with a long-forgotten nest of rotten eggs and a mummified rat.

Thinking about it, it seemed that the book would be closer to the house, maybe stuck back under the steps or poked up over the mudsill, but he had no better luck there than in the barn.

Brushing the dirt off his shirt and pants, Danny sat on the bench by the pepper tree and put his mind onto it again.

Forsythe had only had a few minutes. He'd

never been out to the ranch before so he didn't know any special cubbyholes. What would he do?

He sat right here on this bench, holding the book and waiting for Cisco to come out. Danny turned and put his hand on the first crotch that divided the trunk of the tree, and looked around the yard.

That's probably what he did, Danny thought, turning around to look for a place, leaning against the crotch.

Right then a shiver went up his spine because he knew darned well where that book was.

Making sure no one was watching, Danny climbed the tree, using the familiar footholds.

The calfskin-bound book lay on the bullhide platform, as good as new. Probably Forsythe had thought Danny would find it right off and naturally give it to his mama.

But so many different things had been happening, Danny hadn't had time to go up and dream as he usually did.

Back down at the big table, he opened the book to the first page.

Sur Basin Brand Registry
Property Uvalde County Recorder

On the next page came the brands and earmarks recorded for their general area. The Flying

W with overbite ear crop, the Drag Y with an overslope, the Spear Bar with an oversplit, the Diamond N with an under half crop, the Box B with an undersharp, and on down that page and the next and along the way, Danny saw the 71 of Pat Hare with an upper halfcrop, and the Lazy H with the overhack. Each brand and ear crop and where they were placed on the critter was described and alongside was the name of the brand's owner and where he lived.

The last brand recorded was the Windowpane BB, with a plain cropped ear.

It was so simple. The Lazy H fitted right into the Windowpane, and the plain crop meant most of the ear was cut off, which would take most other earmarks along with it, including their overhack.

Danny ran his finger across the line to the owner of the Windowpane and read: Lance Ballantine, Sur Forks, Texas, and the Windowpane Cattle Company, 310 Liberty Avenue, Philadelphia, Pennsylvania.

Lance! Danny couldn't believe it for a couple of seconds because it didn't fit.

"I'll take that, Dan."

The muddy drawl came directly from behind Danny's back and he slammed the book shut as he jumped with instinctive fear.

"What you so jumpy about, pard?" Lou drawled as he came around to Danny's right side, his hand reaching for the book.

Catching him by surprise, Danny jumped off to the left with the book in his hand, running like a scared jackrabbit.

Lou made a dive at the boy and fell over the bench he'd just been sitting on, giving Danny head start enough to break for the barn, running like the hounds of hell were after him.

Catching up, Lou reached out to grab the boy by the collar, but his long-shanked spurs tripped him and Danny ran through the wagon door of the barn.

"Cisco!" Danny yelled, scooting around the mangers and stalls, out the side door, and back across the hard-baked yard by the bunk-house.

Lou was right on his tail again, cussing a blue streak, but just as Danny felt his hand touch his shoulder, Lou fell on his face.

Danny looked back and saw Cisco standing at the hitch-rail, dallying the reata that he'd lassoed Lou's ankles with.

Lou lay in the dirt, trying to twist free.

In a second Lou would have his .44 out and Danny couldn't think past that.

"Inside." Cisco gave Danny a push into the bunkhouse.

The vaquero followed right after the boy, and dropped the bar over the door that'd take a longhorn bull to break down.

"What is all this?" Cisco asked calmly. "A man

can't hardly have a siesta around here anymore without somebody going loco."

"The book—" Danny choked out, holding it up and gasping for breath.

"Yes, that's the book." Cisco opened it to the last entry. "Looks like Lance was goin' to surprise your mama." He shook his head wonderingly. "What you think?"

"It doesn't make sense." Danny shook his head as Lou began cussing and banging on the door.

"We better do something for sure," Cisco said slowly, scratching his head and frowning. "That feller's gettin' mad."

As he bowlegged it over to the iron stove in the middle of the room, Cisco tore out the last entry page, folded and put it into his back pocket, then he tore out a blank page from the back. Scratching a phosphor on the stove, he carefully set fire to the blank page, saw that it was burning well, then tossed it into the stove.

"Take it easy!" he yelled at the barred door. *"No le hace, no hay prisa, calle te,* I'm comin'."

He had the funniest little smile on his old, weathered face.

Unbarring the door, he stepped aside as Lou came bulling in, his six-gun ready.

Lou looked around the room, glared at Danny, sniffed the smoke, and looked in the stove. He crumbled the ashes between his fingers, and seeing the book in Cisco's pudgy hand, he holstered the .44 and grabbed the registry.

Flipping through the pages, he found where the final entry had been torn out, ran a blunt finger over the torn edge, nodded to himself, looked at Danny with disgust on his chubby features, and said, "So you burned it, you little snot . . . thanks."

He might have said worse, except for the hoof-beats they heard coming toward the house.

CHAPTER 12

TALL AND DREADFUL in his gray mask, Dave Cameron rode, his horse now a burly-shouldered chestnut gelding that showed the sweat stains of hard, long miles.

His gray eyes swept over them like a gusty, cold wind, and he swung off the big horse at the water trough with a painful effort.

Taking off his hat, he beat the dust off his pants and Danny could see he was still unarmed.

He saw the book in Lou's hand, and said, "Forsythe's registry?"

"Too bad, they burned the last part of it," Lou grinned.

"*Compadre, no es cierto*," Cisco said swiftly.

Danny could have sworn just then that Dave smiled behind the gray mask, because his eyes changed as the weather lines pinched in.

"That's a load off my mind," he said. "Where is everybody?"

"Mama's in town, and Lance is off somewhere," Danny piped up. "Where you been?"

"Austin," Dave said quietly, which explained why he'd changed horses and looked so rode out.

"We figured you'd just run for cover," Lou said. "You goin' to stay here, better get yourself a shootin' iron."

"You're backin' a losin' horse, Chamberlain."

"Mister, you're runnin' a bluff that I ain't afraid to call," Lou shot back at him.

"It will cost you dearly," Cameron said somberly, "but then, I reckon it should."

"You seem almighty sure of yourself." Lou wasn't smiling. "Maybe Lance ought to have a talk with you."

"Where is he?" Cameron asked.

"Off yonder, lookin' at his cattle," Lou said slyly, and sloped off toward the rear of the house where he'd hidden his horse when he'd sneaked back.

Cameron watched Lou ride off west until he was sure there was no trick, then nodded at Cisco. *"Da me la hoja, por favor."*

Cisco, with that funny, squinched-up smile, fished the folded page out of his back pocket and handed it over.

Cameron studied it and murmured, "That ought to just about do it. May I keep this?"

"Por supuesto," Cisco said. "I don't want it."

"We sure fooled him," Danny said proudly, and Cisco nodded and patted his shoulder.

Then Danny knew he was wrong, and said, "Cisco did it all."

"No, no, you found the book," Cisco said

207

firmly, and Danny reckoned that maybe leveled it off.

It flashed through his mind that he wasn't afraid anymore of this tall gray man with the hidden face. He'd been glad to see him and accepted his authority without even thinking about it.

"What happened in Austin?" Danny asked.

"I visited an old friend in the Cattlemen's Association," Cameron said, "but that's between you and me, understand?"

"I don't talk," Danny said manfully.

"Danny, we're up against some mighty sneaky skunks. It's goin' to take some doin' to put the run on 'em."

"Which ones?" Danny asked, feeling nine feet tall.

"I don't know 'em all, but there's a chance we can rope 'em in a figure-eight loop and bust 'em down hard," Cameron said.

"I can throw the figure eight," Cisco said, "but that ain't what you mean."

"Almost," Cameron nodded. "We're goin' to have to catch 'em by the neck and forefoot 'em in the same loop."

About then Elizabeth drove the buckboard into the yard, with sacks of meal and other staples in the back.

She looked at Cameron coldly before climbing down and said, "You run off. Why'd you come back?"

"Mama," Danny said, "he didn't run off."

"I thought I could count on you," she persisted, "you being a friend of Harry's."

"Ma'am," Cameron said, "I'm doin' my best."

"It's hard to know nowadays who to trust. Just as I was leaving town, they brought Pat Hare in to the Doc. He'd been bushwhacked."

"Is he alive?" Cameron asked.

"He'll live, but he won't be heading up any roundup soon," she said shortly, climbing down from the buckboard while Cisco commenced undoing the team's harness. Danny picked up a sack of flour in both arms and headed for the kitchen.

Danny figured Cameron would tell her about the book when he felt it was the right time. He sure didn't want to be the one to say Uncle Lance was rustlin' their cattle right under their noses.

When he came out, his mama was still hostile and Cameron was holding himself tall and quiet.

"I don't know what all's going on," she was saying, "but I'm not asking favors from anyone."

"You're the head of this ranch," Cameron said.

"I'd sell out in a second if I could find a buyer," she said strongly. "It's all gone to tatters, and I don't even know why."

"It can get better, ma'am," Cameron said.

"Talk's cheap, I'm finding out," she said. "I can't trust you any more than I can trust my own brother."

"You don't have to trust me, just don't get in the way when the bronc starts to buck."

"Course my note at the bank is near due, but Mr. Vibor's being very sweet and understanding about it all."

She wasn't usually sarcastic like that, Danny thought, but the strain of the times was catching up with her.

Cisco put the horses into the corral and hung up their harness while they all went on into the house and Elizabeth started putting the supplies away.

"Weissgut, Vibor, Chamberlain, you . . . ," she murmured, shaking her head despairingly.

"I'm sorry, but I'm going to have to give you some more bad news," Cameron said.

"I tell you, mister," Elizabeth said fiercely, "any kind of news so long as it's the truth will be mighty welcome."

"Danny found the book." Cameron brought the folded page from his breast pocket.

"Where?" she asked the boy, like he was another one of her tormentors.

"Up in the pepper tree," Danny said, backing up.

"I'm sorry for speaking sharply, Danny." She stepped forward and gave him a little hug. "I swear I'm getting the flutters from being whipsawed back and forth."

Cameron unfolded the page and put it into her hand.

"What ever . . . ?" she muttered, reading down the list of brands. "The Windowpane's registered to Lance and some Yankee company?"

"Lance and his friends have been building up a herd with that brand. He didn't tell you?"

"No, he didn't, but if he had, I'd have wished him well. I always wanted him to get out on his own."

"He's not exactly on his own. He's got that company for a partner."

" 'Course that could be anybody . . . ," she said, handing the page back to Cameron, "maybe he found a financial backer back East to get him in the cattle business."

"Ma'am, your Lazy H fits into that Windowpane so easy an orangutan could make it with a running iron stuck up his backside."

She blinked and swallowed, not wanting to face what anybody could see.

"You're suggesting Lance is overbranding *our* cattle?"

"Yes'm, and all the mavericks he can find."

"Pat Hare said something about a strange brand over on his range."

"I reckon they're not satisfied with just cleaning you out," Cameron said.

Elizabeth sat down on a chair and covered her eyes.

"That does account for a lot of the puzzlements that have been nagging my mind," she said softly.

"Poor Lance, always wanting to play with the big boys."

"We saw the overbrands that first day we rode over toward the river," Danny said, making sure his mama knew it was true.

"Well, for pity's sakes, why didn't you tell me?"

"I wasn't sure how the land lay just then," Cameron said.

"Well, shoot," Elizabeth exclaimed, her eyes still wet, "I'd have given him some cows if that's what he wanted. I suppose he was just too proud to come out and ask for a few hundred brood cows. Proud. Just like our daddy . . ."

Danny could see Cameron was holding back telling her that it was a lot worse than that. She'd forgot a man had been tortured and killed.

"It's warm in here, don't you think? Let's sit outside under the arbor," she said. "I'll make some coffee."

She didn't want to think any more, any deeper. Just learning that her brother was stealing her cows was about as big a shock as she could take right now.

They went out to the arbor, and she fired up the old stove, put on the coffeepot, and said to Cameron, "I can see how difficult it has been for you, getting involved in sticky family affairs, and I'm much obliged for your kindness."

"We're not done yet, ma'am," Dave Cameron

said somberly. "You're goin' to have to be stronger'n you ever thought of."

"I can handle it from now on. It's just a little family misunderstanding that we'll thrash out quick as a catbird. I don't want to shame him, for sure."

"Ma'am—" Cameron started to caution her, but gave up.

As she dumped the ground coffee into the pot and moved it to a back lid, they saw Lance come riding in with Drum Biggers and Clete de Spain alongside. Lou Chamberlain wasn't with them.

"You're just in time for a cup of fresh coffee." Elizabeth stood up, trying to remain in control, and went out to meet the men. "Come right on in and set down."

The three of them dismounted and stepped into the shade. Biggers and de Spain kept Lance in the middle and slightly ahead of them, like he was not exactly their friend, almost as if he were their prisoner.

They eyed Cameron and when they noted he was unarmed, they relaxed a little.

"I'm afraid my little surprise for you isn't going to happen the way I'd planned," Lance said right off, like he had to get it off his chest quick.

"I've had some inkling of it, Lance," she said, "but we can discuss family business later on."

She commenced pouring the coffee and passing the sugar bowl.

"I reckon we've got to talk about it, Beth, 'cause we're starting a drive north in the morning."

"A cattle drive? Well! That's splendid," she exclaimed, but there was little cheer in her face.

"I just—" Lance tried to tell her, but it wasn't easy.

"He's tryin' to tell you that you might be wonderin' what happened to your cattle," Biggers rumbled.

"I already know a number of the cattle have been overbranded," she said, looking at Lance, hoping he'd speak up.

"I guess you might call it a road brand," Clete de Spain chuckled.

"I wanted to wait another week when we were fully prepared to go," Lance said, "but my drovers have decided we'd best leave right away."

"You mean while you can," Cameron spoke up.

"This is none of your concern," Lance said.

"What are your plans for your sister's cattle?" Cameron asked the main question.

"We happen to have private information," Lance said, "that a cattle broker named Joe McCoy will buy every head of cattle we can drive to Kansas. I heard the railroad's moving West from Wyandotte. It'll be clear to Abilene by next spring. If we start tomorrow we'll be settled up there before the first blizzard. We'll winter the herd in the Big Pasture and sell 'em to McCoy in the spring."

"Who's ramroddin' the drive?" Cameron asked.

"I am," de Spain said. "We've got a full crew fresh up from El Paso."

"Everything about it sounds fine, except for changing the brand," Cameron said pointedly.

"My partners wanted to do business with me, not my sister," Lance said. "Besides, the bank already owns a good portion of her stock." He turned to Elizabeth, "Don't you see? That was the surprise—I found a way to save your herd and your ranch."

"So you registered the Windowpane brand with Forsythe, and Biggers's men used the Lazy H catch pens and branded everything—Lazy H, your neighbors' mavericks, and drove 'em on over the river to Biggers's holding ground." Cameron laid it all out in plain language.

"How did you know?" Lance looked at Cameron, then nervously at de Spain and Biggers.

"I rode a big circle one day," Cameron said. "It looked like you'd gathered close to three thousand head. And that's why you couldn't stand to have a roundup. There just aren't enough Lazy H cows left."

"Yes, but it's all for a good cause," Lance protested. "Next spring I'll bring home enough money to buy us a nice place in New Orleans."

"You goin' on the drive, Biggers?" Cameron asked.

"No." Biggers shook his blocky head.

"Likely you'll hire another crew out of El Paso and gather more cattle for another drive."

"That's my business," Biggers said shortly.

"It figures, though. You plan on cleanin' out the whole basin before anybody knows what's happenin'."

"You just about talked yourself to death already," Biggers growled.

"I don't see why it couldn't have been out in the open and let our neighbors get rich at the same time," Elizabeth put in quickly. "It's always been that way."

"That's why I didn't confide in you! You never would let me make any decisions around here. If I'd told you, you'd pick the whole plan apart and nothing would ever get done."

"Maybe I have been overprotective, Lance," she said, shaking her head wearily.

"Now you have to admit that I've done a first-rate piece of work all on my own!" he exclaimed, his cheeks rosy with excitement. "Puny little Lance is going to make us all rich!"

"What's the split?" Cameron interjected.

"It's quite simple," Lance said. "Drum and Clete are being paid by the number of cattle delivered. After that I take forty-nine percent."

Danny wondered why they never really

answered the question of changing the brands.

And why were they taking Lazy H cattle ahead of Biggers's? They could have rounded up the Bar B a lot easier and they wouldn't have needed to change any brands.

For all of Lance's jabbering like a jaybird, something wasn't ringing true.

"Did you get a receipt from Forsythe?" Cameron put in casually.

"My partner will have it. Don't worry, we haven't missed a trick," Lance said, gaining confidence as he talked.

"What's worrying you, Lance?" Elizabeth asked the next hard question. "Why is Lou Chamberlain dogging you? And these . . . gentlemen?"

"We don't want him to get hurt, ma'am." Biggers smiled through his thick beard. "After all, those cattle are in his name. Something happens to him, we won't get paid."

Danny wished he could see Cameron's face. Something was working through his head even though he wasn't saying much. His eyes would look off at the mesquite land like he was working out moves on a checkerboard, then he'd say some little thing and go back to his puzzle again.

"Nothing's going to happen to me." Lance laughed. "I'm lucky."

"So these men are working for you?" Elizabeth asked. "They do whatever you say?"

"Not exactly . . ." Lance's smile faded some. "My partner worked out the arrangements with them."

"I think we better get movin'," Biggers said. "You wanted to say good-bye to your sister and we let you do it. You're done talkin'."

"I know what I'm doing," Lance snapped in a low voice.

"More secrets?" Cameron murmured.

"Mister, you been a burr in my blanket ever since you rode in," Biggers growled.

"Workin' as a brand inspector before the war," Cameron said casually, "I guess I picked up the habit of askin' questions."

"Likely they'd hire you again if you was to go ask 'em," Clete de Spain said, baring his broken yellow teeth in a sly grin.

"I was talkin' to my old boss the other day," Cameron nodded. "He said if my face ever healed up he'd take me back."

"When you figure that'll be?" Biggers asked contemptuously.

"Maybe never, the way you boys play," Cameron said. "I'm in no hurry though."

"Maybe you better get in a hurry," Biggers growled. "You'll live longer."

"Not here," Lance said quickly. "If you want to fight, go down behind the barn."

No one noticed that Danny had slipped off into the house. His little .36 was still safely under

218

his pillow, and he examined its clean lines in the light coming through the window. He rubbed the silver inlay on his shirtsleeve to make it shine, and looked at the silver butt plate that was all engraved with fancy flourishes and feathers, and rubbed that, too, on his sleeve.

He slid the revolver into its holster, then slipped the holster onto his belt.

In the back of his head was the notion that if the big men were going to have a fistfight, he would make sure Biggers and de Spain didn't kick Dave Cameron while he was down.

It seemed like Cameron was chasing a couple of bears with a switch, and he'd end up the same way he had the last time, plumb coldcocked and ready for the stomping.

Quietly, the boy wandered out and took his stool again. They were all looking at Lance as if waiting for a big pronouncement.

"Once we're started north," Lance said, "there'll be peace in the Sur Basin forevermore."

"You haven't told us who your partner is, Lance," Elizabeth asked. "Who do we know in Philadelphia?"

Lance paled and his two guardians shifted their feet and glared at him.

"You must have seen the book—" he stuttered, then looked at the boy. "Danny, did you read that book?"

"Windowpane Cattle Company, 310 Liberty Avenue, Philadelphia, Pennsylvania," Danny said right back at him.

"Danny's very good about his lessons," his mama said, "but who is the Windowpane Cattle Company?"

"I can't tell you," Lance stammered.

"They mean to kill you, Lance," Cameron said. "Your partner will take it all."

"How? Why?" Lance stuttered nervously and started coughing.

"I bet he controls fifty-one percent, doesn't he? Once you're gone from here, there'll be an accident arranged for you. It's plain as a looking glass."

"No! They need me!" Lance croaked.

"Why? Think on it. Tell us who your partner is and at least he'll have to answer to somebody if you don't come back."

Lance put the back of his hand over his mouth and finally controlled his coughing.

Turning to Biggers and de Spain, he asked dryly, "Is that the plan?"

"I'm not plannin' nothin' except makin' sure you go with the drive."

"It would work, wouldn't it?" Lance muttered to himself, working through the new idea. "Easy enough to get rid of me. Maybe that's why he wanted so much secrecy. By God, Cameron, you're right! If I don't go, he'll just sell the cattle and take all the money. If I do go, he'll put me down and take it all anyway."

Cameron nodded slowly.

"Goddamn it!" Lance howled, "Why can't anything go right for me?"

"The only chance you've got is telling us who's pulling the strings," Cameron said flatly.

Unbeknownst to anybody, Danny had his hand on his Colt. He could feel the tension building between the men, only now they were talking life and death, not just a rough-and-tumble fight.

"Thank God you're on our side, Cameron," Lance chattered on excitedly, "maybe it's not too late—"

"Shut up, damn you!" Biggers yelled. "I said, shut up!"

Smiling, Lance moved away, still chattering, "I told you I was lucky. You know that sneaky . . . ?"

Right then, even before they heard the distant shot, a heavy slug smacked Lance in the midsection, blowing his backbone out and slamming him against the log wall of the house.

CHAPTER 13

THE RIFLE SHOT came from the cottonwood grove down by the slough. The next thing Danny knew, Dave Cameron had grabbed him and his mama and dragged them down behind the old pepper tree.

"Stay there!" Cameron said sharply, and hurried to Lance.

Lance's pale face looked like it was carved from beeswax. He'd been so unprepared for death, his graven eyes stared at the heavens in unwavering disbelief.

Biggers and de Spain looked at each other, as surpised as anyone.

"Fetch a blanket," Dave Cameron said to Elizabeth when he heard hoofbeats going away to the south.

Tall and dreadful in his gray mask, Cameron advanced on Biggers and de Spain.

"Who's paying you?" he demanded. "Who set this up?"

De Spain dropped his hand to the butt of his Colt. "Put on a gun, mister, before you start raggin' me!"

"Clete's right," Biggers said. "You got no say-so at all until you can fight like a man."

Cisco came hobbling on his aching, bowed legs, and took one look at Lance. Meeting Elizabeth at the door, he took the blanket from her hands and gently spread it over the body.

Elizabeth stood in shock, her mouth open, her eyes staring at everything, seeing nothing.

"Mama!" Weeping, Danny ran over and hugged her.

He heard Biggers tell de Spain they'd better get into town. Then his mama bent her head down, kissed his wet cheek, and patted his shoulder.

The two mounted their horses and rode out without looking back.

"Danny!" Cameron spoke quickly. "Saddle up. I want to know who they report to. Watch yourself until I catch up."

Elizabeth knelt by Lance as Danny trotted off to the corral for Topsy. He had a glimpse of her lifting the blanket and smoothing Lance's fine yellow hair with such tenderness he was still crying until he mounted up. A man with a horse between his legs can't cry.

The pair of riders weren't trying to hide their tracks and they aimed straight down the trail toward Sur Forks, making his job easy. All he had to do was lay back so far they wouldn't see him through their own dust.

Topsy had to reach out for a long canter to

keep up with Biggers and de Spain, but he was rested and grained, and could carry the boy's weight easily. They were husky, heavy men and their mounts were common broomtails that were easily winded.

The men rode into the main street and Danny brought Topsy down to a slow trot, giving them plenty of lead, trying to blend in with the dusty street and the shacks on the outskirts of town.

He pulled up when he saw them tie their horses at the hitchrail in front of the Merry Widow, and he held back until he saw them cross the street on foot to the bank on the corner.

They climbed the steps and went inside. Joab Vibor was inside that bank.

Danny fingered the .36 Lou had given him.

Bitterly, Danny thought about the whole dirty scheme that Vibor had cooked up with the connivance of de Spain and Biggers to rustle the cattle and ruin every rancher in the Sur Basin. Forgetting about Lou Chamberlain, he wondered if he should go into that bank, catch the three of them by surprise, and blow them all to hell.

Cameron had told him to wait, though, so he would. If Cameron didn't punish them, he would.

He tethered Topsy up the street from the bank, in front of Marshal Gant's office. The old marshal was sitting there as usual, shaving curls off his whittling stick, the big Dragoon slung over his shoulder.

Danny thought about telling him about Lance, but Cameron hadn't said anything about calling in the law.

"Afternoon, Marshal," Danny said, touching his hat.

"You're a mighty small tadpole to be totin' that shootin' iron," Gant said, keeping his attention on whittling off a long curl from the stick.

"I ain't no tadpole," Danny said, and took his time crossing the street, walking as tall as he could.

He sat on the front step of Wilson's Harness Shop, staying in the shadow and keeping an eye on the bank.

After a couple of minutes, Danny figured he'd better move before old Ogden Gant got the notion he wasn't behaving normal and threw him in jail.

He moseyed up the boardwalk and stopped to look in the window of Weissgut's Mercantile, and just when he felt Gant's eyes boring into his back again, Biggers and de Spain came out of the bank and crossed the street to the Merry Widow.

Danny wished Cameron would come. Aware that old Gant was watching him even if he was peeling his stick, Danny turned down the side street out of his sight, then crossed over and went up the steps to the veranda of the saloon, which was screened by latticework.

Kneeling on the bench by the barred window, he could see de Spain and Biggers facing each

225

other inside, talking. Tom Fortune stood clear down at the other end of the bar like he knew better than to try to listen.

"I say we light a shuck while we can," de Spain said in a low but determined voice.

"And leave three thousand head rounded up and ready for the trail?" Biggers said scornfully. "Hell, tomorrow we'll have 'em movin' north."

"You know how slow them longhorns travel. All these folks is goin' to be red hot and smokin' when they hear about another bushwhackin'."

"The way you handled Forsythe is what riled 'em up," Biggers grumbled.

Peeking through the latticework, Danny could see old Marshal Gant slaving over his whittlin' stick, then out at the edge of town he saw a stir of dust that after a minute revealed a rider dressed in gray riding a chestnut horse.

Just to fool old Ogden Gant, Danny scrambled down the back way and sauntered up the side street to the corner half a minute before Dave Cameron rode up at a walk. He'd come hard, but from seeing him on the street, you'd think he was just drifting through.

Cameron turned down the side street, dismounted, and tied his chestnut at an empty hitch-rail. Danny hurried back to him and asked, "You know where they went?"

"I have an idea but I want to be sure," Cameron said, his gray eyes deadly serious.

"The bank," Danny said. "Then they came out and went into the Merry Widow."

"Vibor?"

"Still in the bank."

"Good work, Danny. My notion is to rattle the truth out of 'em all and then turn 'em over to the law."

Danny shook his head. "Two of 'em are gunmen. You can't help Mama if you're dead."

Cameron's eyes went flat. "Danny . . . ," he said, trying to come to grips with something deep inside, "Danny, the gun isn't the right way."

"Maybe not, but right now it's the only way."

"Gant will help." Cameron frowned and gripped his hands together like he was wrestling with his own personal Satan.

"The marshal won't lay down that whittlin' stick until it's all over. The only one who'll help you is me."

Cameron glanced down at the small colt on Danny's hip and said, "You're not going in there."

"I aim to kill Vibor," Danny said, dead serious. "He tried to make a whore out of Mama."

Cameron winced as if he'd been quirted across the face, and his eyes screwed up with the effort of trying to figure out a less violent way. He shook his head slowly, then looked over his shoulder at Joab Vibor trotting across the street, carrying a pigskin briefcase.

Cameron spoke sharply to Danny. "You stay out of this."

He went back to the chestnut and pulled his gunbelt from the saddlebag. It had been rubbed down so long with a rag and tallow it shone like it was alive. In the holster was a short-barreled ivory-butted Army colt, the steel worn to the color of silver, and the old grips a shade of amber.

Hefting the belt, he said, "Danny, try to learn something out of all this, something sensible."

"It's more my fight than yours," Danny protested stubbornly.

"Listen to me, son," Dave squatted down so he could look Danny square in the eyes, "I don't want you to even touch that gun, understand?"

"It's my gun," Danny frowned. "If you don't do the job, I will."

"Stay here," Dave said sharply. "That's an order."

Buckling the old Colt around his waist, he left the boy and went slowly up the front steps.

As Danny hurried back to his bench on the veranda, he saw that Marshal Gant had gone inside, probably for his dinner.

Cameron came in the batwing doors and paused a second to let his eyes adjust to the gloom, then sauntered toward the four men standing at the bar.

There was no sound in the room except for Cameron's boot heels striking the plank floor.

Tom Fortune broke and scuttled out the back door.

That left three facing one.

"Now don't start anything, Cameron," banker Vibor said gravely. "I'm unarmed."

"You started it last year," Cameron said.

"And I'm goin' to finish it," Biggers growled.

"Not till I get the truth out of this two-faced skunk," Cameron said, tapping the banker's pigeon breast with his index finger. "You own the Windowpane Cattle Company?"

"No, sir," Vibor came back strongly. "The shareholders of the First National Bank of Texas own that company."

"And you're the major shareholder in the bank?"

"It's all according to law. There's nothing illegal about it," Vibor said quickly.

"Answer me, weasel."

"Yes, I'm the major stockholder in the bank."

"In fact, the only stockholder."

"Even so," the banker protested, "it's simply business."

"So with your partner, Lance Ballantine, dead, you think you own all the Windowpane cattle?"

"There's no thinking about it. The First National Bank of Texas now owns those cattle without any doubt whatsoever."

"Did you record the brand?" Cameron asked quietly.

"Of course. Mr. Forsythe took care of it."

"But he didn't give you a receipt, did he? Otherwise, you wouldn't have had Forsythe tortured to death over the missing registry."

"You don't know what you're talking about."

"You try to lay claim to those cattle with the doctored brands, somebody's going to string you up to the nearest tree."

"I've had nothing to do with any brands. I employ men who may sometimes make mistakes, but the First National Bank of Texas does not rustle cattle!"

Biggers and de Spain edged apart, planning to draw on Cameron when the time was right and ride off with three thousand longhorns no matter who owned them.

"Why didn't you register that brand in Austin?" Cameron asked, backing up a step.

"It's not required by law," Vibor said, "as long as it's registered locally."

"You don't have a shred of title. Without Forsythe's registry, your word is worthless. The cattle belong to Elizabeth Hamilton."

"I'd hate to see that nice lady and her boy go the same route as her brother went." Biggers grinned.

"I figured you might get that idea, Biggers," Cameron said, backing up another step so as to keep them all in view. "You'd sluice the whole family just to get that herd, wouldn't you? That's why I put on the gun," Cameron said, legs spread, left boot forward.

"I don't give a damn . . . Take him, Clete!"

De Spain suddenly threw himself to one side, quick as a scalded cat, diving to the floor and rolling as he drew to force Cameron into a cross fire.

Cameron's draw was so smooth and fast. His first shot smacked de Spain's forearm as his six-gun came clear. His second bullet slammed into de Spain's head and exited through his neck.

Biggers used the free second to draw and fire at Cameron from the side, but he was too eager and his bullet smacked through Cameron's lower thigh, knocking him sidewise, crashing into a chair.

Holding the Colt close to his midriff as he went down, firing and falling, Cameron's .44 slug caught Biggers in the right hand, blowing the thumb off, and sending the gun flying. With his fourth shot, Cameron punched fur out of Biggers's cowhide vest and slammed him back against the bar.

Biggers drew his spare Colt with his left hand and fired wildly twice as he fell to his knees, and Cameron punched him again, this time in the middle of his bull neck just below the beard, tearing his throat out. Blood spewed from the wound as Biggers fell forward with his head twisted around, flopping loosely in the saw-dust.

Dave Cameron grabbed his leg with his left hand as he slipped to the floor, sucking in a great breath of air.

Joab Vibor sneaked a big-bored derringer from his coat pocket and hurried toward Cameron, meaning to get close enough for a sure shot.

Cameron half rolled away and fired, the bullet smacking Vibor below his belt and angling up through the belly and lung and out through the back ribs.

Through the haze of gun smoke, Danny saw Cameron lay down his empty Colt and hold his upper leg with both hands while the wounded banker flailed about on the floor. Blood was everywhere, puddling and leaking through the cracks in the plank floor.

Suddenly the back door was filled with a stocky figure ambling to the back of the bar.

Lou Chamberlain looked over the silent, crumpled figures, reached under the bar, and lifted Tom Fortune's double-barreled sawed-short Greener.

He broke the breech to check the loads, snapped it closed, and strolled around the bar into the room, never taking his eyes off Cameron.

"You forgot to reload," he said, his drawl knee-deep in Mississippi mud, an innocent smile on his broad face.

232

"What's your interest in this business, Chamberlain?" Cameron swung his body around to face the shotgun.

"My interest is winner take all, and bless the last man on his feet." Lou smiled, showing his dimples. "I reckon that sweet little lady'll have a soft spot in her heart for a hard worker like me."

"She'll make sure you hang," Cameron said strongly.

Wide-eyed, Danny knew he should be doing something, but he was unable to move. For all his pride and secret thoughts of showing off with the gun, he couldn't bring himself to lift it free and use it. Sweat glistened on his face as he fought the battle within himself. "Draw and fire!" an inner voice commanded, but was countermanded by another voice saying, "You can't shoot Lou, he's your friend."

"Why'd she want to hang a sweet feller like me?" Lou said, teasing him.

"Because you killed her brother," Cameron replied.

"And enjoyed doin' it, too." Lou smiled. "The silly blabbermouth thought we were friends."

Lou Chamberlain's words destroyed any loyalty the boy had felt toward him. Lance had trusted Lou, but Lou had fooled him all along, then bushwhacked him in cold blood just when Lance was ready to see right from wrong.

"It was a nice shot for four hundred yards," Lou added with some pride.

With his mind settled and his doubt put down by Lou's boasting, Danny slowly drew the Colt and raised it to the window.

His hand was shaking so bad he couldn't hold a sight. He doubled his left hand over his right and tried again, but it wasn't any better. He wasn't afraid of being hurt, he just couldn't shoot a man without giving him warning.

"You meant to pick them all off one at a time and end up with the jackpot," Cameron said, stalling for time.

"You're the only one could figure that out," Lou said, cocking back the rabbit-ear hammers. "Now I'm goin' to make an oozy corpse outa you all—"

"Lou! Don't!" Danny yelled desperately, and as Lou swung the two-bore around at the window, Danny's hand steadied, and like it was a lesson, he set the pearl button on Lou's left shirt pocket like a moon resting on the blade sight that fitted right in the notch, and squeezed the trigger. The pearl button remained untouched, but a bloody rose bloomed on Lou Chamberlain's lower right chest.

Staggering toward the window, Lou saw Danny frozen there, the little Colt ready to fire point blank between the wooden bars.

"My old pard . . . Lou lifted the two-bore, saw

Danny's determination, and drawled, "I could, but I won't . . ."

Danny squeezed the trigger again, because he didn't trust him anymore.

The whole town was swarming with men shouting, horses bucking, and women howling useless questions, when Elizabeth and Cisco came racing down the street in the buckboard, scattering dogs and loose chickens and anybody foolish enough to be in the way.

Danny stepped back from the window and, still holding the six-gun loosely at his side, saw the townspeople gathering to gawk at the building, but not daring to go inside.

His mama ran up the steps and threw her arms around him. Only then was he able to open his hand and release the Colt. When she was convinced he was all right, she ventured inside the saloon.

Through the window, Danny saw her look around at the silent bodies with her hand over her mouth, then she saw Cameron propped against the far wall, holding his leg.

"Dave!" she ran over and knelt by him, looking into his eyes, then down at his leg.

Cisco was the next to come in and Cameron said, "Cisco, can you put a cinch around this leg, *por favor*?"

Cisco yanked a piggin' string out of his back pocket, knelt down, made a quick tourniquet, and tightened it up until the bleeding stopped.

"That's some better," Cameron said tiredly and wiped his bloody hands on his pants.

Marshal Gant stood at the door, surveying the carnage and said to Cameron, "I suppose you got a good explanation for all this. . . ."

CHAPTER 14

"WE'LL PUSH 'EM HARD the first three days," Cameron said to a rangy, flat-eyed puncher as they went over plans for the cattle drive. "I'd hope we could make eighteen, twenty miles north the first day so's they forget where they've been."

Maybe he wasn't a hundred percent healed, he thought, but another day of idleness like the past week and a half would drive him loco.

"We'll do her," the puncher said, nodding. "I'll pass the word to the rest of the hands."

"I'll be along after a while," Cameron said.

The lean puncher nodded and rode out.

Cameron stepped down from the gray and limped over to the brush arbor, where Elizabeth was fixing a breakfast of fried headcheese, fresh eggs, and a whole loaf of new bread.

She put a platter in front of him and a smaller one for Danny and filled Cameron's coffee cup, then thought a minute to be sure she hadn't forgotten anything.

"Sit down, Elizabeth, please," Cameron said. "I'm against slavery."

"What will the neighbors say?" Elizabeth teased as she sat down next to him.

"They'll think your ankles have broke down," he answered, poking a forkful of crispy head-cheese up under his mask. "Or your hocks are tender from ring bone."

"Dave," she said seriously, "I want to go along."

"Lady, I've got a dozen hands, a hundred horses, and three thousand cows to move clear up to the middle of Kansas. That's a handful."

"Please, Dave," she said softly.

"There's Danny's schooling"—he shook his head—"and somebody has to feed the chickens and milk the cows."

"Danny and Cisco can handle things, and the cows have gone dry."

"Have you come to terms with the shooting, Danny?" Dave changed the subject.

"I been up in my tree, thinking about it." Danny nodded. "I figure if there'd been any good in that man at all, he wouldn't have been where he was, doing what he was doing."

"Something to that," Cameron said.

"I did give him fair warning . . ."

"And you saved my life. I'm much obliged to you," Cameron said.

"Still, I wish he'd changed his ways and rode on out," Danny said, his voice husky, his eyes looking off at the fading stars. "I'd gladly have

238

given him back the damn gun, and felt lots better for it, too."

Finishing his coffee, Dave swung around and took Elizabeth's hands in his and looked her square in the eyes.

"Elizabeth, the next six months' trailin' and winterin' the herd won't be easy, but there's something else. We all can use the time for healing. Maybe my face'll be presentable by the time I come back. And after you've had proper time to grieve for Harry, maybe . . ."

"Maybe I'll be ready for a fresh start," she said, nodding slowly.

"I will be back," he said, each word full of commitment.

"I'll be up in the pepper tree, looking for you," Danny said brightly.

Dave Cameron let loose her hands, gave Danny's shoulder a squeeze, and mounted up.

Tall and enduring, the man in gray rode north in the ruby light of dawn, leaving the boy to wonder at all the knowing it took to travel so far.

Center Point Large Print
600 Brooks Road / PO Box 1
Thorndike, ME 04986-0001 USA

(207) 568-3717

US & Canada:
1 800 929-9108
www.centerpointlargeprint.com